"It's Time I Took A Wife And Started A Family."

Sara's body jerked at Rand's blunt declaration. "A f-family?" she stammered, blinking rapidly to clear her vision. "You dare to sit there and discuss marriage and children as though you were dispensing orders at a board meeting?"

"Is it the thought of having my child that you find so distressing, or what you'll have to do to achieve that particular ambition? Strange," he mused, his eyes knowing as they searched her face, "from the messages those sultry eyes of yours have been sending out over the past couple of years, I imagined you a willing pupil. Was I wrong, Sara?" he murmured. "Haven't you ever wanted me to make love to you?"

Dear Reader,

Welcome to Silhouette! Our goal is to give you hours of unbeatable reading pleasure, and we hope you'll enjoy each month's six new Silhouette Desires. These sensual, provocative love stories are both believable and compelling—sometimes they're poignant, sometimes humorous, but always enjoyable.

Indulge yourself. Experience all the passion and excitement of falling in love along with our heroine as she meets the irresistible man of her dreams and together they overcome all obstacles in the path to a happy ending.

If this is your first Desire, I hope it'll be the first of many. If you're already a Silhouette Desire reader, thanks for your support! Look for some of your favorite authors in the coming months: Stephanie James, Diana Palmer, Dixie Browning, Ann Major and Doreen Owens Malek, to name just a few.

Happy reading!

Isabel Swift
Senior Editor

SDRL-7/85

NICOLE MONET
Rand Emory's Woman

Silhouette Desire

Published by Silhouette Books New York

America's Publisher of Contemporary Romance

SILHOUETTE BOOKS
300 E. 42nd St., New York, N.Y. 10017

Copyright © 1985 by Noelle Berry McCue

Distributed by Pocket Books

ISBN: 0-373-05228-6

First Silhouette Books printing August, 1985

10 9 8 7 6 5 4 3 2 1

America's Publisher of Contemporary Romance

Printed in the U.S.A.

Books by Nicole Monet

Silhouette Desire

Love's Silver Web #2
Shadow of Betrayal #39
Passionate Silence #62
Love and Old Lace #133
Casey's Shadow #177
Rand Emory's Woman #228

NICOLE MONET

an inveterate writer of romances, lives in California with her husband and daughter and makes her writing a full-time career. "I write," the author says, "because I am a voracious reader, and I feel that in some small way I'm paying back all the pleasure I've received in my lifetime."

1

Sara Benedict lethargically replaced the telephone receiver in its cradle and summoned up a faltering smile for the gentle woman at her side.

"Rand?" Edith Hastings inquired, the lines at the corners of her eyes deepening as her brows rose to emphasize her curiosity.

Sara nodded. "He wants me to meet him for lunch."

"How nice of him."

Sara heard the approval in Edith's voice and frowned. "*Nice* isn't a word I'd use to describe Rand," she said. "*Commanding* sounds more appropriate."

Edith's attitude was plain as she waved the bedraggled gray dustrag she held in her plump hand, shaking it vigorously in the general vicinity of the younger woman's face. "You know Rand's thinking only of your welfare. It'll do you good to get away from this house. You've hardly set a foot outside since Sam's funeral."

At the sound of her father's name Sara winced visibly and rubbed the chilled flesh of her upper arms with trembling hands. It had been Bob Hastings, Edith's husband and her father's business partner, who had broken the news to her of her father's heart attack. Bob was a rotund, jovial man who had always reminded Sara of a bald Kewpie doll. But on that particular day the usual twinkle in his kindly brown eyes had been missing, his aging features stark with grief.

Sara shivered. In her mind's eye she watched herself being guided from a house which was no longer a home, stunned and nearly incoherent with the pain of her loss. Bob had taken her to Edith, and they had both given freely of their care and affection during the days preceding the funeral. They were still giving, their generosity undiminished by the discovery that Samuel Benedict, a man they had trusted, had used the firm he owned jointly with Bob as collateral on a loan without the other man's knowledge or approval.

It was Rand who finally forced her to go on with her life. The violent emotions he made her feel had nothing to do with the love she once thought she felt for him, and she had reacted unwillingly to the stimulus he provided. She was grateful for his unemotional expertise in arranging the funeral and settling her father's affairs and yet resentful of the contrast his smooth efficiency was to her own shattered ego.

Sara drew in a shaky breath and clamped her jaws tightly together to put an end to the trembling of her lips. The slight movement showed a vulnerability she couldn't allow herself to feel. She was no longer young and naive, and she did not believe that life held only happy endings. Rand wanted to keep her a princess in an ivory tower. Somehow she had to make him see that she was no longer his Cinderella and the slipper he offered did not fit.

It seemed strange that she should feel such anger and resentment toward a man who, she admitted grudgingly, deserved only her respect and gratitude. Rand Emory was a scion of the San Francisco business community as well as an elite member of the city's social hierarchy. Born to rule the financial empire founded by his maternal grandfather, John Phillips, he had been raised with strict regard to his eventual position in life. He was educated at the most prestigious of Eastern boarding schools, with every step of his schooling rigidly supervised by his grandfather.

Over the years Sara had gained the impression that his parents, two of the "beautiful people" who jetted around the world looking for new and exciting ways to spend the allowance the old man provided, neither knew about nor particularly cared to take an active part in their son's future. They had done their duty by providing an heir to the Phillips millions, and had gone on their way regardless of the bewilderment and hurt their small son must have felt at their neglect.

But, possibly because he had learned early in life to suppress his emotions, Rand had developed a relentless drive that carried him far in his grandfather's affections. After graduating from Harvard with honors, he assumed control of the family business without a ripple of dissent from the other members of the board of directors. The firm prospered under his direction, expanding and diversifying until the Phillips Corporation was among the most powerful companies in the state. The result had produced a man Sara respected for his business acumen and yet feared for the power he wielded. Rand was too dominant a personality to be anything but a threat to her future, she thought.

Edith had resumed dusting the contents of the china cabinet, which was her pride and joy, and as Sara studied her, she noticed the telltale shadows of sleeplessness beneath her friend's eyes. Sorrow and worry were leaving their mark. Quickly excusing herself, she escaped into her bedroom and sat on the edge of the bed. "Sam," she murmured aloud, "why did you do it?"

She didn't have to search long for an answer to her question. After making several unwise investments, Sam had jeopardized the financial security of the firm to continue her education. Her mother had died when she was barely three years old, and from that day on there had just been her and Sam. He had always wanted her to have nothing but the best, she thought sadly. They had been everything to each other, which was why, when Sam was so abruptly wrenched from her life, even the compassion provided by Bob and Edith hadn't been able to lessen the pain that was still tearing at her soul.

"Oh, Sàm," she whispered. "Did you feel the bars closing around you the way I do? Was that why you left me alone?"

Sara's mouth set in determination as she rose tiredly to her feet. She glanced at the bold black and white face of the alarm clock beside her bed. She had agreed to meet Rand for lunch in less than an hour, and she wanted to kick herself for giving in to his wishes with such a lack of gumption.

But she hadn't always been reluctant to be with him. At the thought, Sara flushed and moved jerkily across the room. After gathering together clean clothing, she hurried down the hall toward the bathroom. Yet even an increase in activity couldn't stem the flood of memories, and she gave in to the inevitable as she stepped beneath the soothing spray of the shower.

The first time she saw Rand she was sixteen, with a head stuffed full of romantic daydreams. Her father had met the younger man at a political fund-raising dinner, and despite the difference in their ages the two had become good friends. Rand became a frequent visitor to their home, and on many nights Sara had curled up on the couch in their living room to listen to discussions ranging from the state of the world to baseball.

Looking back, she realized her hero-worship had been inevitable. She listened to every word Rand said, watched every movement of his lean, well-muscled body, and generally made a nuisance of herself. But a man nearly fourteen years her senior had the maturity she lacked and understood the fervent emotions of a young girl in the throes of her first real infatuation. With a sensitivity she hadn't appreciated at the time, he showed her affection while still keeping a certain aloofness. His gentle teasing was calculated not to wound her budding femininity, and he never showed a trace of amusement for her obvious devotion. He also, much to her eventual relief, had never taken her seriously!

Maybe that was why her current attitude toward him held so many emotional nuances, she thought. In Rand's estimation, any nineteen-year-old female just finishing her second year of college automatically required guidance. Since Sam's death she had been left in no doubt of Rand's intentions. Because of the friendship he had shared with her father he would accept responsibility for her, since he imagined she was far from able to do it for herself. Well, Rand Emory was certainly going to have his eyes opened to the truth, she decided.

Anger guided the force of her grip as she shut off the flow of the shower and lent an added sparkle to her eyes as she roughly toweled herself dry. An unamused laugh pushed itself past her lips as she stepped into delicate lace underwear and hurriedly pulled a spaghetti-strapped sundress over her tousled hair. She was a capable adult. She wasn't going to accept Rand's plans for her future. She wasn't going to give in to his dominance, and she certainly wasn't going to let him assume Sam's role in her life!

Sweet, biddable little Sara had been buried with her father. Whether he liked it or not, Rand was going to have to cope with the woman who had emerged from her grief. That woman now had a purpose—to repay the sacrifices Sam had made for her. Only then could she live with the finality of her father's death. She was going to make sure Bob Hastings didn't lose the business he had helped to build, and at the same time she would keep her father's name from being sullied in bankruptcy court.

As she finished dressing, Sara wondered why Rand hadn't asked her to meet him at his office in San Francisco's bustling financial district. Instead, his instructions were to take a cab directly to one of his favorite restaurants off Mason Street and to mention his name when she arrived. She didn't want to discuss the plans she'd made for the future with a roomful of strangers looking on, but maybe it was for the best. She anticipated Rand's anger, but knew him well enough to know that he wouldn't make a scene in public.

Sara found it difficult to leave the warm security of Bob and Edith's home, but once she arrived at her destination she became interested in her surroundings and was relieved to discover some of her nervousness dissipating. The restaurant was a lovely Victorian restoration of the original 1906 landmark, a visual feast of early San Francisco history. As she climbed the stairs and entered the imposing building, she discovered the inside to be as pleasing as the exterior. Exquisite antiques enhanced the old-world charm of the building, and as she crossed to the reception desk her heels clicked rhythmically against the white-tiled floor.

She was led immediately to a corner table set aside from the other diners, and at the sight of Rand lounging at his ease in a cane-bottom chair her nervousness returned. His face wore a shuttered expression as he watched her approach, and as her gaze dropped to the table she noticed his fingers tighten around the glass he held.

"I hope I'm not late," she murmured.

He rose to his feet as the waiter seated her, his voice noncommittal as he replied, "We're not running a race, Sara. Relax, and at least try to enjoy yourself."

Bristling at his indifference, she asked, "Is that why you arranged to meet me here and not in your office? If so," she concluded ungraciously, lowering her eyes to her hands twisting uneasily in her lap, "you're wasting your time. I'm not in the mood to be entertained."

Rand sat and leaned forward to tap Sara's cheek sharply with one finger. When her startled gaze rose he drawled, "Act your age, Sara."

She flushed at the rebuke and was relieved when their waiter chose that moment to return to their table. The menu was still unopened beside her, and with relief she heard Rand ask for permission to order for her. Nodding her compliance, she felt the faint breeze from an overhead fan cool her cheeks. To escape from his brooding scrutiny she sought out the whirling blades and caught her breath at the lavish detail of the embossed metal ceiling.

"A lovely distraction, isn't it?"

Unaware of the pleasant expression replacing the anxious one, she returned her attention to Rand. "It's beautiful."

Her relaxed countenance seemed to please him, and his hard, rather austere features softened as he whispered, "Do you know how much I've missed seeing that smile on your face, my sweet Sara?"

The smile he admired faltered and then completely disappeared. A frown knit Sara's brow as her eyes registered confusion at the unaccustomed note of sensuality in Rand's voice. The air seemed suspended in her lungs as his gaze caught hers, as they were captured by each other's allure. She didn't see the other heads in the room turn to glance at them, but the curiosity of the scattered diners was inevitable. Rand and Sara were both tall and black-haired and had an intriguing air of isolation that caught and held the attention. This striking couple seemed to be in a world of their own. But the contrasts between the two were what fascinated many in the room into a breach of good manners.

Rand's high cheekbones, straight aquiline nose, and full-lipped but stern mouth lent him a hawklike appearance. The bones of Sara's heart-shaped face were more fragile, her nose retroussé, and her mouth as soft and vulnerable as a child's. Where Rand was tanned from the sun, Sara's complexion was creamy-white, with the natural bloom of a dusky pink rose on her cheeks and lips.

As the silence between them lengthened, Sara noticed Rand's eyes lower to her mouth. She felt the impact of his glance like a touch and squirmed uneasily in her chair. At once his attention shifted and again she lost herself in the piercing depths of his stormy gray eyes. She couldn't break away from the spell he wove so effortlessly. She saw his hand move, as though in a dream, and reach for her fingers, which were unconsciously tracing the design in the white damask cloth covering the table.

"Sara?"

His velvet growl broke her free of her mindless fascination, and his hand tightened when she attempted to free herself from his touch. Her skin burned where his probing thumb slid against her palm, and her whole body shook in reaction to the heat he generated. "L-let go of my hand, Rand," she stammered nervously, suddenly aware of the interest they were arousing. "People are staring."

"You're worth staring at."

This time the sweep of his eyes acknowledged no boundaries, and she shivered as his attention focused on the rapid rise and fall of her chest. "Are you getting a kick out of embarrassing me?"

He shook his head abruptly, his gaze hardening as he stared at the rebellious slant of her mouth. "When are you going to stop fighting me, honey?"

As he spoke he released her hand, and Sara

hurriedly replaced it in her lap. She frowned with puzzlement at the inflection of defeat in his voice and forced a meaningless smile on her face as she answered him. "I've never fought you."

His mouth quirked wryly. "Never, Sara? Then why do you refuse to let me make good your father's debts?"

Her lashes lowered to shield her expression. "Because as Sam's daughter, repaying his creditors is my responsibility."

Rand viewed her defiance with a disgruntled mutter as he surveyed her discomfiture with ill-concealed impatience. "I'm not going to argue the rights of responsibility with you. Sam was my friend, and I once promised that if anything happened to him, I'd look after you."

"I didn't know that," she said, finding it almost impossible to control the tears demanding release at yet another indication of her father's worry over her. "But it doesn't make any difference. I wish you'd stop badgering me."

Sara's last words were a pitiful appeal for understanding, but Rand hardened himself to the pleading expression she wore. "There's no reason for you to worry unnecessarily, Sara. It would be sheer lunacy to tie yourself down to a debt it would take you years to repay."

"Isn't that my decision to make?"

Sara could see the negative response to her question on his face, but before he had a chance to speak their waiter returned with their meal. Consciously willing her tense body to relax, she unfolded her napkin. Placing the linen cloth in her lap, she eyed the filet of beef, which was accompanied by fresh garden vegetables simmered in cheese sauce. What little appetite she might have had vanished, wiped away by the frustration she could feel coming from Rand.

The waiter departed discreetly, and she felt her tenseness increase. In an attempt to delay further conversation, she began to cut into her meat with feigned enthusiasm. To her relief Rand followed her lead and attended to his own meal in grim silence. Somehow Sara managed to continue eating long after her stomach began to revolt, and it wasn't until Rand asked her if she'd like dessert that the strained quiet between them was broken.

"No, thank you."

Rand beckoned to their waiter, his lips tightening at the childish primness of her refusal. She heard him order two cups of coffee and waited in dread as their table was cleared. As she had suspected, once the waiter placed their coffee in front of them and left, Rand lost no time in resuming their earlier discussion. There was no hesitancy in his manner when he leaned forward in his chair, his features cool and composed.

"There's an easier way to solve our problem, Sara."

The intensity of Rand's gaze pinned her to her chair, and she shifted uneasily. "I fail to see any problem," Sara insisted, her mouth firming with irritation. "Last week I talked to Mr. Phelps, the loan officer at Sam's bank. After the sale of the house goes through and I pay off the mortgage, there'll be enough money to pick up the arrears on the remainder of my father's business loan."

"And just what are you going to do then, write a letter to Santa Claus like a good little girl?" Rand's hand rubbed against the back of his neck, his irritation evident. "For God's sake, be realistic! That second loan your father took out by using his firm for collateral greatly exceeds the first. The bank is not a charitable institution, and they aren't going to be held off by your winsome appeal for very long."

"I will make the required payments to the bank."

"And just how do you expect to do that?"

"I've been majoring in business administration at the university. With two years of instruction behind me, and excellent grades in all my courses, I shouldn't have too much difficulty."

She heard the hiss of his indrawn breath. "Too much difficulty doing what, Sara?"

"I intend to quit school and go to work as a secretary."

"Like hell you'll quit," he exploded, a muscle pulsing angrily against the taut flesh of his jaw. "I'm going to finance the rest of your education as well as repay any company losses incurred by your father's loan. When I get back to the office I'll phone Phelps, and—"

"You will not!"

When she rose shakily to her feet he looked surprised and then enraged by her refusal to go along with his demands. "Sit down," he ordered, his hands gripping the edge of the table unconsciously.

Feeling curious stares boring into her back, she returned to her chair, but her own eyes flashed in a face suddenly pale. She'd never had Rand's formidable temper directed at her before, and now she fully realized how accurate the rumors regarding his ruthlessness had been. Until this moment she'd known only gentle consideration from him, although it was often mixed with an irritating degree of indulgence. But then, she'd never tried to thwart the great man's wishes, she thought waspishly.

Gathering together her scattered courage, she met his anger in the only way possible, with her own. "You have no right to order me around, Rand Emory. You're not my father, and I'm not one of your lackeys!"

"I'm not suggesting I play the role of a parent," he responded dryly, having used the time gained by her outburst to reestablish his self-control. "I have a different relationship in mind, Sara. I suggest we marry. As my wife you would have no reason to object if I chose to repay my late father-in-law's debts."

Her heart plummeted directly to her stomach as she stared at him incredulously. "What did you say?"

With a sardonic quirk at the corner of his mouth he replied, "You heard me."

"You surely aren't suggesting that I . . . that we . . . ?"

The curve of his mouth deepened into a vivid slash of cynical mockery. "Why shouldn't we marry, honey? You feel a responsibility to pay Sam's debt to his partner, and I feel a responsibility to you. It's the most sensible solution to the problem, can't you see that?''

Had Rand always been this cold and calculating? she wondered in amazement. How could she have blinded herself to his true character for so many years? Being referred to as a responsibility was bad enough, but Sara nearly crumpled from the pain of having a marriage between them referred to as a "sensible solution." She stared at him as she would at a stranger. Outwardly he was still Rand, the man she had once thought she'd love forever. But as she met his cold, emotionless gaze, she realized she had never looked past the handsomely distinguished face in search of the man inside.

She had been blinded by his kindness to her and seduced by the warmth of his eyes into forgetting who he really was. Rand Phillip Emory, she thought, his name reverberating over and over in her mind, as though by repetition she could cast aside the man of her imagination. He had been reared from the cradle to accept responsibility as a necessary part of his life, and now she had become just that to him . . . a responsibility.

She was nineteen, a woman of charm and intelligence, yet in Rand's eyes she was only the orphaned offspring of a friend. She knew her behavior since her father's death hadn't exactly stressed her maturity, but surely a man with Rand's perception should be able to make allowances for her grief. Lifting her head, she studied his features and quailed for a moment. His eyes were narrowed, and his mouth was compressed with annoyance. There wasn't a trace of real emotion in his carefully controlled expression, and with a shiver she realized he made allowances for no one . . . least of all her.

"Dammit, Sara, don't look so horrified."

"What were you expecting . . . me to fall all over you in joyous relief at the thought of becoming your wife? I'm sorry to disappoint you, Rand, but I have no intention of becoming a puppet to add to your collection."

With an exasperated expulsion of breath he stiffened. "I'll admit to your youth and innocence, Sara, but I've never had to question your intelligence. You're lovely enough to please the most discriminating tastes, and it's time I took a wife and started a family."

Her body jerked at his blunt declaration. "A f-family?" she stammered, blinking rapidly to clear her vision. "You dare sit there and discuss marriage and children as though you were dispensing orders at a board meeting?"

"Is it the thought of having my child you find so distressing, or what you'll have to do to achieve that? Strange," he mused, his eyes knowing as they searched her face, "from the messages those sultry eyes of yours have been sending out over the last couple of years, I imagined you'd be a willing pupil. Was I wrong, Sara?" he murmured. "Haven't you ever wanted me to make love to you?"

2

Sara glared at Rand. She was nearly choking with rage and humiliation. "What you're proposing has nothing to do with loving, and I refuse to be a part of it!"

"That's your immaturity speaking," he said, his voice revealing his disgust at her behavior. "I'm fully aware that you're unawakened and probably as frightened as hell of the physical side of marriage. But I have no intention of forcing myself on you like an animal, for heaven's sake!"

He struck at her feminine pride with his words, and Sara reacted with indignation. Tilting her rounded chin to a belligerent angle, she retorted, "I am not afraid of lovemaking, Rand Emory!"

"Then why are you getting so hot and bothered at the mere thought of becoming my wife?"

"Is that what this is, a proposal of marriage to the woman you love?" she asked, her head moving from side to side, denying him the opportunity to respond. "I don't think so, Rand."

"I want to take care of you the way Sam would have wanted me to, Sara."

Her eyebrows arched upward in mockery. "You think Sam would have wanted you to provide me with a sexual education?"

"Stop trying to twist my words to suit yourself," he muttered, a dull flush rising in his cheeks. "I want you to be able to live with me without providing the gossip columnists with a field day."

He leaned forward, his voice husky as he penetrated her defenses with a glittering stare. "I promise to give you all the time you need to accept me into your bed, honey. You have nothing to lose and a great deal to gain, Sara."

"Do you place self-respect so low on your list of priorities?"

"What about the respect I have for your father's wishes?"

She whitened at the cruelty of his question, her eyes filling with tears. "Sam wouldn't have wanted me to marry a man who doesn't love me," she said.

Rand groaned and ran a hand through the thickness of his coal-black hair. The gesture revealed his fatigue as well as his frustration. "I care more for you than for anyone else."

"That's not enough for marriage, Rand."

"It's all I'm capable of giving you. Your head may be full of dreams of romantic love, but I'm experienced enough not to believe in such nonsense. Every relationship is based on a certain amount of greed, Sara. We all want something, and few of us care about anything but the end result. Marriage should have both passion and fondness, with each partner honest enough to admit to the advantages to be gained by such an alliance."

"You've damned yourself with your own words," she retorted, barely able to contain her anger. "In your eyes I'm still a child. Passion is the last thing you feel for me!"

His gaze hardened, and he deliberately lowered his eyes to her breasts. For long, heartstopping moments he surveyed her shadowy cleavage. "Give me a bed and you naked in my arms, and I'll show you how wrong you are."

The image Rand's harsh whisper implanted in her brain had the desired result. The elegant restaurant with its well-dressed clientele disappeared, and Sara was suffocated by his unrelenting gaze. She felt a sensation that was almost physical . . . skin sliding against skin, softness yielding to hard masculine contours, a mobile mouth twisting in hunger against her own . . .

Sara's eyes were drawn to that mouth, and she cringed at the small, knowing smile she encountered. His lips were curved in triumph and celebrated the insight that allowed him to cruelly exploit her vulnerability. Realizing how expertly she'd been manipulated, she was furious. Dear heaven, she thought disbelievingly, the man has only to speak and I'm like putty in his hands. But to be forewarned is to be forearmed, she thought, tightening her fingers until her nails dug into her palms. From now on she wouldn't underestimate the power of Rand's physical and mental appeal. She didn't dare!

They left the restaurant together, as emotionally far apart as two people could be. By the time Rand pulled his car in front of Bob and Edith's modest terraced Victorian home, he was grimly silent. To escape from the tension caused by his closeness, Sara stared out of the window. She was reassured by the familiarity of the heavily shrubbed, nearly perpendicular hillside, with its steep wooden staircase that led to the house. She desperately longed to climb those stairs and escape into the haven the Hastings' home represented. She felt drained after venting her resentment during the drive and frighteningly close to tears.

"You won't reconsider?" Rand's voice held traces of harshness as he turned her to face him.

She answered with a look as cool as the one he had given her and shook her head. "I'm not selling myself for the security you could provide, Rand."

"God, you're more of a child than I realized," he exclaimed. His hand clamped around her arm like a vise to prevent her exiting from the car. "Just cool down and listen to me for a blasted minute! I'm not through talking to you."

"But I'm through listening to you being so damned condescending," she snapped, jerking her arm free of his hold. "I've already told you my plans, and you're not going to change my mind by ridiculing them. No matter what you think, I'm perfectly capable of deciding my own future without any help from you."

"Even though you know Sam would have wanted me to help you?"

Her brow furrowed, and she bit down hard on her lower lip to prevent a cry of anguish. "Sam wouldn't have wanted me to marry for any reason but love."

She heard the deep inhalation of air into his lungs, but failed to see the pain darkening his eyes. She was staring down at her hands, watching as her fingers twisted together uselessly. She wasn't prepared for the arms that reached for her, drawing her close to the comfort of his warm body. With a despairing sigh she leaned against him, blocking her mind to the anger between them and responding to him as she had in the past.

"You're right, Sara," he sighed, his breath ruffling the hair on top of her head. "Sam wouldn't have wanted you to marry against your will. But you know as well as I do that he would have wanted me to help you in any way possible. Can you at least accept a job from me, if nothing else?"

She tilted her head against his arm, her eyes wary as she studied his face. "What kind of a job?"

"We have two openings at present," he said quietly. "I'm not going to have you accuse me of manufacturing a position for you, although you're overqualified for work as a typist. But it would be a start, with plenty of scope for advancement."

"And I'll be able to take full responsibility for my father's debts?"

He nodded, and brushed at her dampened cheeks with a gentle hand. "There's only one stipulation I'm going to make, Sara."

"And that is?"

He smiled at the uneasiness of her expression and placed an avuncular kiss on the tip of her nose. "You finish your schooling through evening classes."

Her reaction was immediate. "There's no way I'll make enough money working in a typing pool to pay the bank payments and my tuition. If you intend to pad my salary, I . . ."

"You'll make the same wage as the other typists," he remarked firmly. "No one at the office will know I'm also paying your tuition."

"Because you won't be!"

"The fall semester's already been taken care of, Sara."

"You had no right . . ."

He shifted until his hands clutched her shoulders. She saw his mouth tighten just seconds before he began to shake her. "Don't tell me I have no right. Your father was my friend, and I'm damned if I'll stand by and see his dreams for you go down the drain."

His movements stilled as he saw the rosy color disappear from her face, and he groaned regret for his impulsive actions. But although his hands eased their pressure on her shoulders, his attitude held marked impatience as he once again resumed his speech. "Look, you can consider my assistance to be another loan, if it'll salvage that priggish pride of yours. Although you're not acting very bright at the moment, I know you have more than your share of intelligence. Any promotions you receive within my organization will be earned through your own ability, that I promise you. In matters of business I don't play favorites."

"Isn't paying my school fees showing partiality?"

"I consider it more in the nature of an investment."

Sara sniffed and rubbed the moisture from her cheeks with the tips of her fingers. His voice had held a teasing inflection, and her mouth curved in a conciliatory smile. "If that's true, you're not the astute businessman I imagined you to be."

"Why?" He laughed as he rubbed her shoulders lightly with his palms. "Don't you intend giving me value for my money?"

More disturbed by his touch than she wanted to admit, Sara pulled away. The instant Rand's hands released her she felt regret oddly mingled with relief. She liked being held by him, but she couldn't let herself give in to his charm. In Rand's mind she had become both a responsibility and a possession. He had a need to protect what he considered his own, and considering her emotional state, it would be easy for her to give in to her own need to be cared for.

Straightening against the plush upholstery of Rand's low-slung Porsche, Sara withdrew emotionally from the man at her side. She knew opposition would make him only more determined than ever to bring her around to his way of thinking, and she just didn't have the strength left to fight him. To let him shoulder her burdens was too enticing a prospect; her loneliness of spirit was too acute to afford her any protection from her own weaknesses. She trembled and nervously fingered the strap of her dress.

For Rand to discover how close she was to total capitulation was unthinkable. Far better to compromise, she thought nervously, than to risk losing the concessions he'd already made. But with a surge of rebellion she decided her pride wouldn't be sacrificed for peace. She had come this close to ensuring her independence—surely she could find enough courage to take it one step further. With this thought she half turned in her seat, her features composed as she studied his profile. "Rand?"

He acknowledged the sound of his name on her lips with a smile. "What is it now, you little firebrand? I can tell by that look on your face that you're still spoiling for a fight."

"No," she said, her voice firm as she studied his face. "But if I agree to do as you wish, it's with the stipulation that I pay you back after I graduate."

"There's no need," he began, but quickly faltered in his assertion when he noticed the steadiness of her gaze.

Quick to see her advantage, Sara pressed gentle fingers against the soft weave of his jacket. "I do appreciate what you've done for me, and what you're trying to do," she said with quiet sincerity. "And I don't mean to seem ungrateful. But I have to start making my own decisions and leading my own life. Please . . . try to understand."

Rand's hand reached up to cover hers where it rested against his arm. His eyes, as they looked into hers, held the respect she had struggled so hard to gain. "I can't honestly say I approve of the pressure you're placing on yourself, but I do understand, Sara."

"And you're not angry with me?"

"I'm furious," he said with a smile. "It's not my usual practice to allow myself to be beaten by a feisty stubborn woman with sad eyes. If news of this gets around, stock in my corporation will drop drastically."

She sighed with relief and asked, "When do I start work, boss?"

A finger of light edged through minute cracks in the window shade and made a direct hit into Sara's eyes. As an alarm clock, she thought disgruntledly, that darn shade couldn't be faulted. With a sigh she rolled over, bunching her pillow in her arms as she struggled to fight off the lingering mists of sleep. She studied her surroundings and felt a familiar sense of satisfaction. Her apartment was small, but for her it represented a great deal of personal achievement.

She stifled a giggle as she recalled Rand's face when he'd first visited her new apartment. Admittedly, it had looked quite different a year and a half ago. But putty had covered up the holes in the plaster, and white paint and a few colorful pictures had brightened up the interior. Poor Rand, she thought. When his arguments failed, and he realized the only way he was going to get her out of her chosen home was by the scruff of the neck, he had made the best of the situation. He had ended up working off his irritation since she also refused to let him hire a firm of interior decorators to make the place livable.

This time Sara's giggle escaped wholeheartedly, and she sat up and leaned against one of the large bolsters which, along with a matching slipcover, made her single bed into a sofa during the day. Wrapping her arms around her raised knees, she grinned at the thoughts going through her mind. The images she liked to remember the best were of Rand with speckles of white paint dotting his dark hair, or on his knees, muttering imprecations under his breath as he vigorously sanded the scars and pits out of her hardwood floor.

Stretching her arms over her head, Sara yawned and resisted the urge to lie back and close her eyes. Instead, she focused her attention across the room to the single window set in an old-fashioned ledged casement. Behind the shade a new morning dawned, and if she hoped to meet the challenges it presented, she was going to have to get a move on. Jumping up, she padded across the room on bare feet, eager to see what the winter day had to offer. A simmering excitement brightened her eyes as she stood framed between lemon-yellow drapes, an anticipatory smile on her face as she studied the scurrying figures on the rain-washed pavement below.

Sara acknowledged the reason for the anticipation that gripped her. During the last few weeks she had been acting as Rand's temporary secretary, and although working closely with a man who seemed to suffer from a father complex was an exercise in frustration, she couldn't deny her own enthusiasm. For the first time since she'd started as an employee of the Phillips Corporation, she felt she was working at full mental capacity.

Sara thought back over the last seventeen months. After starting work, the time had passed with unbelievable swiftness. As Rand had promised, she was placed in the secretarial pool as a junior typist. Although hardly stimulated by the work itself, she enjoyed her job. The surroundings in which she spent her days were pleasant. The large central room housing the typing pool was without windows but was saved from starkness by colorful prints on the walls. Rand didn't stint on the comfort of his employees. The office equipment was the most modern money could buy, and the recessed lighting was the best.

As agreed, Sara worked toward her college degree in business administration by attending evening classes. Between school and work she often put in twelve-hour days, determined to prove her ability to repay the money still outstanding on her father's loan. The hours she kept were long, but she welcomed the distraction. Without realizing it, the first throes of her grief were eased by the weight of the responsibilities she shouldered, and needed sleep replaced the tears she would have shed.

Sara found no time for social life. She discouraged the men who sought her company, and she never questioned her decisions. Her days followed a set pattern of work and study, and she allowed herself none of the luxuries she could have afforded with all the overtime she put in. Although Rand accused her of playing the martyr, she lived with what amounted to Spartan simplicity in her studio apartment in a far from luxurious area of San Francisco and bought only what was necessary for her existence.

Much to Rand's disgust, she no longer shopped for clothes to please herself, and Sam wasn't there anymore to urge her to take pride in her appearance. So she dressed in tailored suits and functional blouses she felt fit the image she had of a single-minded career woman, and she learned to believe in that image to the exclusion of everything else. For her, there was nothing else!

That's what she told herself whenever she was with Rand, which was more often than she wanted to be. He seemed to always be hovering in the background of her life, and although she resented his constant surveillance, she soon learned that protest was useless. Rand just couldn't seem to accept her as a capable adult. It was true he had given her a job, but in so doing he seemed to imagine his position as her boss gave him the right to dominate her personal as well as her business life. He criticized her clothes, the way she wore her hair, and lately even found time in his busy schedule to rant at her for trying to work herself to death.

Acting as Rand's secretary certainly hadn't improved the situation, she thought. Even with his office door closed she felt as though he were breathing down her neck. He watched her for the least sign of fatigue and yesterday had actually suggested shortening her hours. Sara sighed and began to gather together her clothes. When was he going to learn that she wanted no special concessions from him?

She considered herself simply another employee, and she wanted to be respected as such. How could she prove her own worth to the company when Rand persisted in trying to wrap her in cotton? Mrs. Burns, his secretary as well as his grandfather's before him, was elderly enough to merit such concern. But Sara was young and healthy, and she hated the way Rand continued to treat her like a child. Lately, she'd been torn between a longing for Mrs. Burns to come back and being depressed at the thought of returning to the typing pool.

With a sigh Sara turned and began to prepare coffee in the alcove that served as her kitchen. The area boasted a chipped sink, an antiquated refrigerator, and a narrow two-burner stove. She was glad to be able to cook her own meals and not have to stretch her meager budget by eating in restaurants. As kitchens went, it was far from attractive, which was why she separated it from the rest of the apartment by a curtain. Unattractive it might be, but it was at least functional.

After the coffee started perking, Sara continued to force her thoughts into a practical direction. She searched the hangers in her closet until she found her favorite outfit—a sleeveless white blouse with a demure ruched collar and a tailored navy blue skirt and jacket. With these over one arm and her toilet articles in the other, she unlocked her door and stepped into the shabby, second-floor hallway of her apartment building.

At first she'd hated the thought of sharing a bathroom, but since getting to know the other occupants on her floor her nervousness had disappeared. There was old Mrs. Tarrant and her cat, Thomas, and Patty, a pert brunette who worked as a waitress at a nearby restaurant. On the whole her neighbors were quiet and friendly without being intrusive.

There was only one exception, she thought with a smile. Six months ago the vacancy in 3B had been filled by a young man who was far from quiet, and who couldn't, by any stretch of the imagination, be counted unobtrusive. Fred Smalley was young, good-looking, and had a winsome appeal that brought him constant attention. His neighbors had quickly welcomed him into their hearts as well as into their homes, Sara included. When Rand arrived unexpectedly one evening to find Fred in stocking feet, comfortably sprawled on her couch, he had nearly succumbed to apoplexy.

Depositing her clothing on a lopsided hook on the back of the bathroom door, Sara laughed out loud. After being introduced to her newest neighbor, Rand had been ready to move her into the nearest YWCA, until Fred batted his gorgeous baby-blue eyes at him and invited him over to his place for a drink. After Fred left, playing the role of rejected suitor for all it was worth, she had laughed until her sides ached.

Sara turned on the shower and winced as air exploded through the pipes. Their building dated to pre–World War II, and the plumbing left a lot to be desired. Unzipping her ankle-length robe, she stepped into the garishly green plastic stall. As she washed she sighed her enjoyment. The pipes might sound like a train rumbling through a tunnel, she thought, but at least there was always plenty of hot water.

Sara dressed, applied a coat of peach lip gloss to her mouth, and had just finished smoothing her hair into the French twist she favored, when she heard a groan from the hallway. She hurriedly grabbed her discarded robe and toilet articles together and unlocked the door. As usual, Fred was leaning against the wall with closed eyes, his curly blond hair standing on end.

"Good morning, darling."

The greeting was a half-hearted mumble, and he winced at Sara's cheerful response. "Been burning the candle at both ends again, Freddie?"

"You're not helping any, Sara."

At his sharp reply, she patted his arm consolingly. "Will you forgive me if I leave you my hair dryer?"

He managed a nod, one eye popping open. "Will Emory be by tonight to check up on you?"

"Not that I know of," she said, an impish smile curving her lips. "Why?"

Freddie's other eye opened, and Sara was treated to a stare of boyish innocence. "Don't be dense, love. I'll have to return the dryer sometime, won't I?"

"When are you going to give Rand up as a lost cause, Freddie?"

Her laughter was silenced when he winked, and he lumbered into the bathroom. "Jealous, sweets?"

Scowling, Sara turned and stomped down the hall. "Don't be ridiculous!"

She had almost reached her door when Freddie bumped into her from behind, nearly propelling both of them onto her apartment floor. "For heaven's sake, what are you trying to do?"

"You forgot to leave the hair dryer."

"You deserve to have your golden locks sticking out like a wire brush," she retorted, shoving the dryer in his hands. "After that crack you just made, you're lucky to have any hair left."

"You're right," he said, his eyes twinkling. "You have nothing to be jealous of. It's you Emory is interested in—if you know what I mean."

Sara felt her cheeks burning, but didn't know whether she was embarrassed or angered by Fred's assumption. "You know very well that Rand is a family friend as well as being my boss. He's not interested in me that way."

"Now who's walking around with their eyes

closed?" he snorted, clutching the hair dryer to his chest as Sara made a grab for it.

Her irritation with Fred seemed to linger through the rest of Sara's morning. Everything that possibly could go wrong did. She broke the heel of her shoe while getting on her bus and had to hobble the two blocks back to her apartment to change footwear. That made her late for work, and her mood wasn't improved to find Mrs. Burns waiting for her with a disapproving stare. After such an inauspicious beginning with Rand's secretary, Sara's usual poise and competence completely deserted her.

She made hash of the file cabinets while trying to find the new accounts she'd recorded during Mrs. Burns's absence. She placed an important client on hold and forgot to signal the call on Rand's extension. This last indiscretion earned her a lecture from Mrs. Burns, and when Rand walked in during it, Sara wanted to jump out of the large plate-glass window set into the far wall. Instead of being a gentleman and leaving her to suffer her fate, he sat on the edge of her desk and listened to every denigrating word Mrs. Burns uttered.

Just once she looked up, to find him studying her bent head. Their eyes met, and when she recognized the expression in his, she stiffened with indignation. The beast was enjoying the novelty of seeing her put in her place, she thought furiously. She didn't bow and scrape in his presence, so he seemed to be amused seeing her at a disadvantage. Well, he hadn't stayed amused for long, she remembered with satisfaction. Not an hour later she'd taken him his morning coffee, tripped, and flung the contents of his favorite mug all over his desk. But her ineptitude took its toll. By the end of the day she was ready to do battle with the nearest available victim. It was just his bad luck it happened to be Rand.

3

Sara pressed a hand against the small of her back as she trudged up the stairs to her apartment. Her body ached, her head hurt, and her legs felt like leaden weights as she finally reached the landing. She couldn't remember ever spending such a miserable day, and all she wanted to do at the moment was shower and fall into bed. If the hunger gnawing at her insides couldn't be helped by a slice of toast, she thought tiredly, then her stomach would just have to wait until tomorrow. Since she hadn't eaten breakfast or lunch, one more missed meal wasn't going to kill her.

"Sara?"

She turned at the sound of her name being hissed, a frown of annoyance tilting her brows. "Not now, Freddie!"

"You've got a visitor, darling."

Sara's frown turned into a glare after she inspected the empty hallway. "Are you trying to be cute again?"

Freddie tiptoed into the corridor, dressed as usual in skin-tight jeans, thonged sandals, and a garishly colored madras shirt. A little of Sara's sparkle returned as she absorbed his dramatics. Freddie was addicted to television programs that featured suave, debonair private detectives. The way he was skulking about, she couldn't help wondering which of his heroes he was imitating at the moment. There was one thing for sure, she thought fondly, it was hard to be depressed for long around Freddie.

"Scout's honor," he whispered, pointing to the closed door of her apartment. "McCauley let him in."

"Let *him* in?" she questioned, her eyes narrowing with instant suspicion. "Now I know you're playing one of your tasteless jokes on me. Mr. McCauley is too circumspect a landlord to let a man into my apartment."

"Not when the old coot thinks he's your guardian."

"I haven't got a . . ." Sara's eyes widened as her exhausted brain made the connection. "Oh, God!"

Freddie nodded with satisfaction. "The name certainly fits."

"What in the world does he want now?"

"You, I suspect."

"Don't start that again, you pinhead!"

He grinned, thoroughly unrepentant. "You'd better hurry and face the music. If the look on his face was any indication, you're in for it."

Sara grimaced and glanced nervously over her shoulder. "Did he look angry or furious?"

"On a scale of one to ten?"

She nodded, and Fred, a natural mimic, assumed a forbidding expression. He looked so much like Rand at his worst that she groaned. "I think that's a ten and a half."

"At least you know what to expect, love."

She turned away, straightening her shoulders as she walked toward her door. "Thanks, Freddie."

Rand's icy tones lashed out before she had time to close the door behind her. "Where in hell have you been? Do you have any idea of the time?"

Thank goodness she'd been warned, she thought, sending a silent prayer of gratitude winging Freddie's way. If she'd been confronted by Rand without time to gather together her defenses, she would have probably succumbed to a seizure on the spot. Instead, she sauntered over to the sofa with studied insolence, and glanced at her wristwatch before propping herself against the cushions. It had stopped at eleven-fifteen, but she wasn't about to admit it to Rand. "It's a little after seven-thirty," she guessed.

"A little after is right," he snapped, moving to stand in front of her with legs spread wide and his hands on his hips. "An hour and a half after, to be exact. This is your break before the spring semester, so you don't have school as an excuse."

Thinking that Rand's appearance was putting an appropriate end to a dreadful day, she replied rather more flippantly than she ordinarily would have when he was in this kind of mood. "How clever of you."

"Where have you been, Sara?"

The tightening of his lips should have been a clear enough warning, but Sara chose to ignore the storm signals flaming to life in his penetrating gray eyes. "I don't think that's any of your business."

With a growling exclamation she was dragged unceremoniously to her feet, and the hands that clutched her shoulders were inescapable bonds. "Should I ask whom you were with?" he drawled, his teeth grinding together after the question was uttered.

Sara's eyes widened as she realized the extent of Rand's fury. She was having trouble understanding the reason behind his loss of control. This wasn't the first time she'd been insolent, and certainly it wasn't the first time she had scorned him for interfering in her life. Usually, he returned her sarcasm without ever giving her the satisfaction of knowing she had gotten to him. So why, she wondered, was tonight different? What could she have done to generate this degree of animosity?

"Well, are you going to answer me?"

A combination of a pounding head, exhaustion, and hunger caused her to sway into the strength of his body. She was grateful for his tightening arms, even though their strength held no tenderness. With a sense of inevitability she heard herself giving him the explanation he demanded, at the moment too tired to argue her rights to privacy.

"You've been working all evening?" he asked incredulously, cupping her chin with one hand while his other arm supported her head. "In heaven's name, why?"

She tried to smile, but her mouth only trembled in response to the commands from her brain. "I made a real mess of things today, and since I'll be returning to the typing pool tomorrow, I wanted to get everything in order."

"What makes you think you'll be returning to the typing pool?"

She gave him an exasperated glance. "You won't need me now that Mrs. Burns has returned."

"Ahhh, now we get to the purpose of my visit," he murmured, grinning when her eyes widened and she stiffened against him.

"Rand, will you quit teasing me and tell me why you've come?"

"I was going to talk to you this morning, but you were rather . . . ummm . . . preoccupied."

At his snide reference to her dressing down by Mrs. Burns, Sara flushed. "Yes, and you enjoyed yourself immensely, you beast!"

"Anyway, you were in such a temper, I decided it prudent to let the dust settle before asking you if you'd like the job as my secretary on a permanent basis."

"What?"

He laughed at her incredulous squawk. "Before you arrived this morning Bertha handed in her resignation. She's well over retirement age, and it seems her doctor has finally convinced her to take things a little easier."

45

With shaking hands Sara clutched the front of his shirt, excitement flaring in her eyes. But when she saw the indulgence in his expression, she lost much of the pleasure she felt at the thought of continuing as his secretary. Instead, she found herself questioning his motives. Why should she be offered the job when there were others in Rand's employ who had greater seniority? Was he using this opportunity as a means to keep her under closer scrutiny, and to prevent her, as he recently accused, of "working herself to death"?

The thought rankled, and her retaliation was swift. "I'm certain there are others with more seniority who are qualified for the position, Rand."

"In June you'll have your degree in business administration," he countered, his voice heavy with displeasure at her reaction. "I once said you'd earn any advancement through your own merits, and I meant it, Sara. You're overly qualified for the work you're doing for me at present, and you know that as well as I do."

Her chin tilted defiantly. "Is it so easy to read my mind?"

"Hell, yes," he said, his voice holding a bitter inflection that shocked her. "But I'm not going to argue with you. Do you want the job or not?"

"Of course I want it, but I . . ."

"You and that damned pride of yours!"

"Why shouldn't I question your motives?" she asked, shoving her hands against his chest. "Since you're constantly harping at me for being childish, how in the world am I expected to believe you actually find something about me to admire? My hesitation was that of any responsible adult considering an advancement, and yet it makes you furious to have me question my suitability for the job. Just because you can't control me as you do your other minions, don't take your frustration out on me. I never asked you to be my keeper!"

To her relief Rand released her abruptly and stepped back to look at her with an expression of dismay. "Do you really think I'm trying to control you, Sara?"

She shrugged and turned away from the hurt look in his eyes. "What else am I supposed to think?"

"Why don't we ever talk about friendship and caring in our relationship, honey?" he asked quietly. "I'm at a loss to understand this hostility that springs up whenever we're together. Am I to be blamed for wanting to keep you in my life, when you must know how important you are to me?"

By placing his actions in such a perspective, he made her feel like an insensitive monster. Yet didn't she have sufficient grounds for complaint? she asked herself. All children had to face the tribulations life had to offer if they were to mature. Mistakes were inevitable but necessary to the learning process. In Rand's eyes she was still a child, and yet he seemed to think he could cushion her every fall. He spoke of the dissension between them and wondered why it was there, but suddenly Sara was beginning to understand.

She wanted him to see her as a woman, not as a

child! A woman with all the natural human frailties common to the human race. Instead, she was forced to teeter on a pedestal of his making, not a child but by no stretch of his imagination an adult. She was certain if she allowed herself to be swayed by the force of his character she would lose her self-respect—and lose herself. She didn't want to constantly fight him for her emotional freedom because she knew the damage that would be done to their relationship. She needed to retain her own identity, and yet she loved Rand too much to want him to disappear from her life.

Rigid with shock, Sara finally acknowledged the truth that she had buried for so long. Because her feelings for him were different from those she'd felt as a young and awkward teenager, she had convinced herself that the love she once felt for him was a figment of her schoolgirl imagination. The lethargy and depression caused by her father's untimely death had only reinforced this delusion, when in actual fact the opposite was true. Now she could fully understand why Rand's attitude so infuriated her.

Because of the peculiar circumstances behind their relationship, his particular code of honor wouldn't allow him to view her as he would any other reasonably attractive female. If office gossip were to be believed, Rand led a far from celibate existence with the women of his acquaintance. Since his affairs were of short duration, she suspected he related to women solely on a physical level. If so, it wasn't any wonder that he had trouble placing her in a convenient category. It was safer to keep her a child in his mind than to risk being attracted to her sexually.

And yet, she was certain that he was as physically drawn to her as she was to him. Only moments ago he had held her in his arms, and now she speculated on the reason for the increased tension she had felt in him. She had heard the accelerated throb of his heart as she pressed her ear to his chest, a rousing beat she now recognized as a familiar sound. Right now, couldn't she feel its matching rhythm pounding in her own breast?

"Are you all right?"

Sara heard his voice, saw his worried glance as he studied the paleness of her face. But somehow, when she looked at him, his familiar features were nearly those of a stranger. Why had she never noticed the disturbing sensuality that emanated from him with every movement of his body? she wondered. How could she have guarded her mind for so long against the aching need to touch him, to press her mouth against the dark hair protruding from the V of his shirt, to smooth his warm flesh with her hands? She trembled as he approached and bit down on her lip to keep from crying out when he reached for her.

"Honey, what's wrong?" he questioned abruptly. "Are you ill?"

"Rand, I . . ."

Her eyes looked avidly at his face. Her shaking increased as her whole being responded to the impersonal touch of his hands. So this was desire, she thought in amazement as she felt herself lifted in his arms. With a cry she burrowed her face against his throat and inhaled the heady aroma of his clean, masculine body. She knew by the burning of her cheeks that she was no longer pale, and she needed to hide her reaction to him until she had time to understand it herself. Dear God, I don't want to love him, she thought bitterly. I don't want to love anyone!

"When did you last eat?"

As he spoke Rand laid her on the sofa and gently adjusted a pillow for her head. The prosaic question brought with it amusement verging on hysteria as she acknowledged the irony of the situation in which she found herself. Here she was, with every nerve cell riotously attuned to the prospect of intimacy, and he was concerned with the condition of her stomach.

"I had dinner."

His brow quirked wryly. "Tonight?"

Shamefaced by her weak attempt at subterfuge, she averted her eyes. "Well, no, but I . . ."

Rand's only reply was a curse uttered under his breath.

Sara looked at him reproachfully. "You needn't swear at me."

"Somebody has to keep you in line," he said, shaking his head in a despairing gesture. "You need someone to watch over you."

Sara clenched her hands into fists. It was infuriating how easily he could slip into the role of stern parent guiding a recalcitrant youngster. But old habits could be broken, couldn't they? Immediately, any desire she might have had to restrain her emotions until she was better able to handle them disappeared. Her thoughts were tempting in themselves, and she moistened her dry lips with the tip of her tongue as her body responded instinctively to his closeness. She watched his eyes follow the movement, and she felt the quick, sweet expulsion of his breath against her mouth.

The sensation was as evocative as the kiss she hungered for, and she immediately lost the will to resist. She needed to make him as aware of her as she was of him. He was seated beside her, his hands braced on either side of her head as he watched the hardness of her expression melt. With a rapidly beating heart she locked her hands against the back of his neck and smiled up at him.

"How closely do you need to watch over me, Rand?" Her fingers moved against the hair at the nape of his neck. "I should imagine that with a handful like me it would have to be . . . very close."

His eyes narrowed on the provocative pout of her lips. "You little devil, are you flirting with me?"

Sara boldly increased the pressure of her hands. "And if I am?"

"It's a very dangerous game, sweet Sara."

"Isn't it better than fighting all the time?"

She saw the movement in his throat as he swallowed and knew a moment of triumph. But her elation was short-lived, as Rand unlocked her fingers from around his neck and stared down at her as he straightened up.

"It would be if I thought you could cope with the inevitable conclusion." Rand shook his head angrily.

"You little fool," he uttered harshly, his eyes scathing as he stared at her. "Just what do you hope to get with this kind of behavior?"

Hurt, she responded to his question with anger of her own. "I thought you wanted our relationship to be more . . . affectionate," she chided him, pushing herself into a sitting position as she returned his scornful glance in full measure.

"And you think this is the way I expect you to show me you care," he exclaimed, running a hand through his hair in exasperation, "by offering me your body?"

She flinched. "I wasn't, I . . ."

He was unrelentingly grim as he shook his head. "Somehow, considering you've never been overly concerned with pleasing me, I find your protest hard to swallow."

"You wouldn't if I were any other woman," she argued, frighteningly close to tears as she tiredly laid her head back against the supporting cushion at her back. "I'm not a little girl anymore, Rand!"

"Are you just trying out your feminine appeal on the nearest handy male, then?"

He hesitated, and when he brushed a strand of hair from the corner of her mouth, she sensed the unaccustomed caution in the gesture. Somehow, the wariness in his manner hurt more than she would have believed possible. Already his attitude toward her had begun to alter, and without trust to temper the change, the result could only spell disaster.

It was better if he imagined her a silly kid with overactive glands, she thought bitterly, than a woman in love. If he ever suspected the true state of her emotions, she knew he wouldn't hesitate to use them to gain his own ends. He would renew his offer of marriage to fulfill the obligation he felt he owed her father, and feeling the way she did now, she would most likely be willing to accept any crumbs of affection he chose to offer her.

So Sara decided to retreat, and although she found such subterfuge distasteful, she became the wide-eyed ingenue he had always imagined her to be. She pouted and gazed up at him reproachfully. "You once offered to teach me to make love, Rand. I'm almost twenty-one and still a virgin. I've decided it's time I took you up on your offer."

"When did I make such an offer?" he asked heatedly, a flush darkening the cast of his features.

"Give me a bed and you naked in my arms, and I'll show you how wrong you are, Sara." She recited the words he had once spoken to her with a teasing inflection in her voice. Only Sara was aware of what the effort had cost her.

When Rand threw back his head and laughed, she knew she had chosen the correct method to alleviate his suspicions of her. If she'd been in any doubt, his next words put her fears at rest. "God, you little tease! You really had me going, do you know that? I thought you were trying to get your own back by making me hate myself."

She gazed at him innocently. "Would I do that to you, Rand?"

"In a minute," he replied cheerfully, getting to his

feet. Stretching to ease his tension, he lifted one eyebrow. "Shall I take you out and feed you now? It might mellow that temper of yours. I've certainly had enough of your particular brand of revenge for one evening."

She forced a smile and shook her head. "I really am tired."

He was instantly contrite and brushed a gentle finger across the taut line of her jaw. "Are you certain the added responsibilities of being my secretary won't be too much for you, Sara? I don't want you to feel you have to accept this promotion out of misplaced pride. Your last six months at the university are going to be tough, and I don't want you to overtax yourself."

Sara rose and pulled him toward the door. The hands that grabbed his arm were amazingly steady, considering the anguished state of her emotions. When teasing laughter replaced the sobs she badly wanted to utter, she was nearly convinced that acting was her true vocation. "I'm not worried," she remarked cheerfully, giving him a cheeky grin. "I can do anything you care to dish out with one hand tied behind my back. Anyway, if past performance means anything, you'll throw me out of the office headfirst if I try to work a minute past five o'clock."

He twirled an imaginary mustache as he opened the door. "Simon Legree at your service, madam."

"Oh, go home," she said, pushing him into the hallway.

Her voice must have held more desperation than

she'd intended to convey, because Rand's expression immediately sobered. "Promise me you'll eat something and get right to bed? You really look at the end of your tether, honey."

Sara kept the smile on her face until he had disappeared down the hall. Her head was pounding in earnest now, and the thought of food sickened her. Locking her door, she turned out the lights and threw herself across the sofa without bothering to undress. In the comfort of darkness she no longer had to play a role. She was the woman who ached with loneliness and who longed to have loving arms holding her close. She could cry as she hadn't since her father's death and know there was no one but herself to hear the sound of her anguish.

4

Sara had just returned from lunch and was putting her purse in the bottom drawer of her desk when Rand's voice lashed out at her. "Sara, where the devil did you put that contract I was going over this morning?"

"Good afternoon to you, too," she mumbled indistinctly, straightening and fixing him with a look of controlled impatience.

"Burroughs Construction?" she asked.

Rand's jaw looked as though it were clamped as tight as a drum, his eyes hostile as he nodded. Without waiting to remove her coat Sara walked to the file and opened the top drawer. It took her only a moment to scan the alphabetical listings before she located the missing contract. Placing the bulky folder in Rand's hands, she returned to her desk without tossing him another glance.

She couldn't trust herself to look at him. If she did, she might be tempted to tell him what she thought of his behavior over the last few months. He constantly found fault with her, and she was getting heartily sick of always being on the defensive with him. The only praise he handed out was impersonal, usually in regard to her work. He didn't seem to find anything else about her to admire, and the knowledge ate away at her self-confidence. Also, since that memorable evening at her apartment nearly six months ago, he avoided any contact with her outside of the office.

Sara soon discovered that for her, heartsickness was an incurable disease. She went about her tasks during the day with seemingly calm efficiency, but whenever Rand was around, her insides twisted with nerves. She had lost weight, but her lack of appetite was only one of the symptoms of her affliction. Another was recurrent insomnia. She had lost count of the number of nights she'd studied herself into numbing forgetfulness when sleep had proved elusive. Well, at least some good had come out of her inner turmoil, she thought, her mouth shifting with visible cynicism. Last week she had received her degree in business administration from San Francisco State University, and had graduated near the top of her class.

But no amount of makeup could hide the shadows beneath her eyes, and the grimness of Rand's mouth when he looked at her lately spoke volumes. She knew he blamed her washed-out appearance on the stress she was under both at work and at school, and it was easier to let him think her a fool for setting herself such a torturous schedule than to have him guess the truth. She couldn't bear it if he came to realize it was desire for him that was burning her up alive.

To add more confusion to an already unbearable state of affairs, her own behavior was filled with contradictions. She avoided any conversations with him that even slightly verged on the personal and perversely hated both him and herself for the lack of communication between them. During the first few weeks after being made his secretary, Rand had sometimes suggested meeting her for dinner during a break in her evening classes. But Sara resented him for his sense of obligation. She used the need to study as a reason to refuse, and eventually the invitations ceased.

No matter how distant they became with each other, Rand never completely forgot his feeling of responsibility toward Sara. His concern only increased her bitterness, and the terrible gap between them widened. When he voiced his worry over her appearance, she reassured him of her well-being with distant impersonality. She needed to be more to him than an obligation. Although she longed for a return of the closeness they once shared, however fraught with difficulty, she made it impossible for him to get through her defenses. Lately, he had stopped trying.

That was what hurt the most. She had what she'd

always wanted, her independence from Rand. In his eyes she had finally grown from a child, but into a person with whom he didn't particularly care to associate. The fault was hers, and yet what else could she have done under the circumstances? Her one unsophisticated attempt to show him how she felt had been met with rejection. She wasn't strong enough to risk a second rebuff.

Yet, no matter how much she wanted to put an end to her torment, her love for him was growing obsessively. Every time he asked her to send flowers or jewelry to his latest girlfriend, she had ample proof of her feelings. Although the names changed frequently enough to reassure her of the casualness of his affairs, only by hiding behind a barrier of reserve could she prevent herself from showing the jealousy that ate at her.

But an inner control born of desperation always held, and she showed little or no emotion as she responded to his requests. Sometimes there was a curious watchfulness in his eyes as he gave her her instructions, as though he sensed her disapproval and was just waiting for her to explode. Although the idea was ridiculous, she suspected Rand took a perverse delight in taunting her with his relationships.

When Rand laid the folder down on top of the gray file cabinet and looked over at her, her irritation grew to gigantic proportions. She wished he wouldn't stare at her like that! As she felt a warmth ripple down her spine, she carefully schooled her features into the calm mask he was used to seeing. But as she glanced down at her hands she noticed with dismay the telltale trembling of her fingers.

Grabbing several new pencils from their holder on top of her desk, she crossed to the electric sharpener fastened to the wall. She needed to keep busy if she hoped to withstand his scrutiny, and this particular task didn't demand a great deal of concentration. Considering the unease she felt in his presence, she knew better than to try to cope with the partially completed reports stacked beside her typewriter.

"Will you put those damn things down? I want to talk to you."

Rand's footsteps were muffled by the deep carpet, and she jumped when she heard his voice directly behind her. The pencils fell from her hand, and with an incoherent mutter she stooped to pick them up. Unfortunately, Rand chose that moment to be helpful. Her eyes encountered the bunched muscles of his thighs as he squatted beside her, their outline clearly visible beneath the straining material of his slacks.

Sara averted her fascinated gaze from his lower torso, but the damage was done. Her nerves were jumping, her senses alive to every aspect of his body. She was aware of the fine black hair on his forearms, the cuffed sleeves of his blue shirt rolled back to aid in her discovery. His scent was heady, a combination of musk-fragranced soap and sheer, earthy male. A fine sheen of moisture dotted her forehead as his breath, sweetly scented with mint, was swallowed by her indrawn gasp as he drew her to her feet.

She spoke hurriedly, praying that her vocal cords would hold up under the strain. "I didn't know you didn't want the Burroughs account returned to the file. When you left here in such a hurry this morning, I assumed you'd forgotten to clear your desk."

"That's not what I want to talk to you about."

His words reverberated above her bent head, and she briefly closed her eyes at the note of seriousness in his voice. "Should I bring my steno pad into your office?"

Rand's hands flexed against the slender bones of her shoulders. She suspected he wanted to shake her for the indifference of her reply, and when he began to remove her coat she almost wished he had. Backing against the wall, she grabbed the lapels before he could slide the material from her arms. "I—I'm cold."

"That's an understatement!"

The coat was off and flung over the back of her swivel chair before she reacted to the ambiguous meaning of his statement. "What is that supposed to mean?"

"Why did you cancel those reservations I made for you?"

"They were made without my approval."

"That's no answer," he countered, his turbulent gray eyes deriding her evasiveness.

With a shrug she whirled around, seeking to evade his inspection of her strained features. "It's the only one you're going to get."

"Is it, by God?"

There was no inflection in the words, but their

impact was strengthened by the quietness of his voice. Sara instantly regretted goading him, realizing her mistake when he shoved her into his office and slammed the door shut behind them. She was guided to the straight-backed chair beside his heavy oak desk, and she sank down onto it without waiting for him to demand she do so. It was a matter of expediency, not obedience, she told herself. Her knees were threatening to buckle, and the last thing she needed at the moment was the embarrassment of having to pick herself up off the floor!

When Rand sat on the edge of his desk, his long legs dangerously close to her knees, she acknowledged the vulnerability of her position. He seemed tense, as though he were readying himself to reach out for her if she prepared to bolt. But Sara knew there was no place to run even if she gave in to the impulse to seek an escape from him. There was no escaping her feelings. Her only defense was in keeping them hidden.

In scathing tones she asked, "Just what do you hope to achieve by this example of egotism, Rand?"

"I hoped to make you see some sense," he exploded.

"What about, the little vacation you planned for me without my knowledge?"

"It wasn't going to be a little vacation," he admitted wryly. "I'd arranged for you to spend a month in the Bahamas as a graduation present."

"Then thank you, but I'm afraid I can't accept your generosity."

"It isn't generosity, it's plain common sense."

He braced both of his hands against the curved arms of her chair and leaned forward until their eyes were level. "I can't rely on the competence of a secretary who's suffering from exhaustion," he said, the clipped tones underscoring his agitation. "You're burnt out, Sara. You need a rest."

"I need to be allowed to put my degree to good use," she argued. "I admit I'm a little tired, but I'm hardly on my last legs. Although I appreciate your concern, I assure you it's not necessary, Rand. I'm perfectly capable of arranging my own leisure hours, and I'll do so when I'm ready and not before."

"And if I make it a condition of employment?"

Her gaze didn't falter at the implied threat. "Then I'll have to start looking for another job."

He straightened, all animation leaving his face. "I see."

She nodded and got to her feet. "Will there be anything else?"

"Not at the moment," he replied dispassionately, his polite tones more than a match for her own.

During the next few days, Sara and Rand went about their work in a state of armed neutrality. Sara was aware of the resentment seething just below the surface of their relationship, and was wary of precipitating what might well prove to be a final confrontation. But emotions too long suppressed have a volatile effect on good judgment, as she soon learned.

Her downfall began innocently enough. For weeks Rand had been negotiating to gain the chairmanship of the Burroughs Construction Company, a family-operated firm with a good reputation but a lack of necessary cash flow. She and Rand had just spent several hours working with both the Phillips Corporation lawyers and representatives from Burroughs Construction, and by the time the bid proposal was finalized Sara was limp with exhaustion. The Burroughs lawyers departed after promising to let Rand know the decision of the board at the earliest opportunity, but Sara knew it was all over.

Rand never left anything to chance, she thought, glancing around the empty conference table after everyone had gone. She began to gather together the notes she had taken of the meeting, her mouth compressed with the strain of the last few hours. Rand had wanted a controlling interest in the Los Angeles–based company in order to expand several pending government-subsidized contracts, and considering the present state of the economy, those contracts were too lucrative for Burroughs Construction to pass up. The family would open their ranks to include Rand, and given enough time and profit they would forget they had ever been independent of the Phillips Corporation.

Sara knew she should be elated at Rand's success, but instead she was depressed. Accustomed to the power he wielded, he never hesitated to press his advantage. The longer she worked for him, the more she became convinced that to show Rand Emory a weakness was to risk becoming completely absorbed by the ruthlessness of his personality. John Phillips had trained him well, she thought sadly as she walked past heavy carved double doors and into Rand's office.

The object of her thoughts looked up as she entered the room, and he watched her approach with an unblinking stare. Expecting him to express satisfaction with the outcome of the meeting, she was disconcerted by the curiously empty look in his eyes. His features were drawn, his mouth compressed. He looked every one of his thirty-five years, she thought.

"You can go ahead and file those," he said, indicating with a dismissing wave of his hand the folders she carried.

Surprised, her brow furrowed in unconscious imitation of his own. "You won't want to go over the changes in the contract?"

"I'm not a damn machine, Sara!"

Hurt by his clipped reply, she retaliated unthinkingly. "You could have fooled me."

"Do I detect disapproval?"

She shrugged and started to turn toward her own office. Before she had taken two steps Rand was on his feet, jerking the folders from her hands. Throwing them onto a corner of his desk with uncharacteristic carelessness, he smiled. "I'm proud of you, Sara."

"What?"

This time the smile reached his eyes. "You handled yourself well through the negotiations. You were charming, confident, and extremely perceptive. I just want you to know how much I appreciate your assistance."

Flustered by his praise, she stammered her thanks. Rand simply shook his head and motioned for her to be seated. Returning to his own chair, he leaned back against the padded leather with a sigh. "I must be getting old," he murmured, grimacing as he flexed his arms in a stretch.

His brown suede jacket was unbuttoned, and the movement stretched his shirt across the width of his chest. Sara swallowed with difficulty. Keeping his hands locked against the back of his neck, he misinterpreted the reason for her involuntary grimace. "Don't you think I ever get tired of the rat race, Sara? I can assure you I do."

Irritated by the teasing inflection in his voice, she retorted, "Then maybe you should take that trip to the Bahamas!"

As soon as the words left her mouth, Sara was appalled by her own stupidity. She couldn't believe she had so thoughtlessly made reference to an issue between them that was better forgotten. The remark seemed to hang in the air, reverberating in her mind like an echo. Rand lowered his arms, and she glanced down at the hands that rested now against the corner of his desk.

She expected him to be clutching the edge in an attempt to control his anger at her insolence, but to her surprise the fingers were relaxed. She frowned her puzzlement, and returned her eyes to his face. Other than a slight compression of his lips, Sara saw no signs of the blowup she anticipated.

"That's the best idea you've come up with all day."

She shifted nervously and moistened her lips with the tip of her tongue. "What is?"

"The Bahamas," he repeated patiently, his eyes widening with assumed innocence. "I haven't played hooky for a very long time. I wouldn't be able to take the full month I'd arranged for you, but I suppose I'm entitled to at least one week in the sun."

A smile of anticipation curved his mouth. "What I wouldn't give for a few days with nothing to work on but my tan!"

The image of Rand stretched out on warm white sand, his nearly nude form soaking up the sun, made her response awkwardly defensive. "You were in Florida less than three months ago."

"Such derision from one so young," he said, a mocking inflection in his voice. "That was business. We were talking about pleasure."

His soft chuckle was as abrasive to Sara's nerves as sandpaper against wood. Stiffening, she tilted her chin before she attempted a rejoinder. "Were we?"

"Why so defensive, Sara? I know you turned down my offer of a vacation, but you can still come with me if you like."

Sara sucked in her breath and glared at him. "No, thank you!"

To her amazement, Rand responded to her belligerence with a distracted air. "You're right," he said. "I'd completely forgotten about the sales convention in Nevada next week."

His exclamation seemed to reflect more tiredness than disappointment, and Sara stared at him in surprise. "You can always go away afterward."

He shook his head, his expression rueful. "If today's meeting was as successful as we think, I'll have to be conferring with the Burroughs family in L.A. roughly two weeks from now. There will be a great deal of time and work involved, and the sooner they get used to functioning as a part of the Phillips Corporation, the better it will be for all concerned."

Oddly enough, considering the years she'd known him, she could never remember Rand showing this kind of weakness. He usually thrived on challenge and became revitalized by the demands his career placed on him. A nagging concern for his welfare tugged at her. Forgetting her earlier acrimony, she examined his drawn features sympathetically. He really does look tired, she thought. In a softened mood, she asked, "Couldn't that be put off for a few weeks?"

He shrugged. "That company's been hanging on by a thread. Any delay in reorganization could cost me a bundle."

"There are more important considerations here than money," she argued, leaning forward to emphasize her point. "You were the one who said you're not a machine, Rand."

"Would you have me ignore my responsibilities, Sara?"

She sighed with exasperation and shook her head. "Of course not! But you could always appoint someone else to go to Nevada in your place."

"Since I'm the one who planned the convention for our sales reps, then I should be there to hand out the awards and see to organizing the various functions."

"Most of the sales representatives and their wives will be too busy enjoying an expense-paid week at the casino to be offended by your absence," she insisted.

Heavens, no wonder the man looks tired, she thought in frustration. What did he expect, when he constantly refused to delegate authority? Irritated by Rand's careless attitude where his own health was concerned, she said, "I can think of several people in your employ who would be competent to handle any last-minute details."

"How about you, Sara?"

"Me?" she whispered, disconcerted by the unexpected suggestion. "But I'm just your secretary."

"I've been toying with the idea of giving you an administrative title and a raise in salary now that you've earned your degree. For quite a while you've been given responsibilities far in excess of those delegated to a secretary, and you know it as well as I do. It's time you were rewarded for your performance, and taking over the convention details can be your first duty as my executive assistant. Does the job appeal to you, Sara?"

Her acceptance was instantaneous, and Rand laughed at the excitement she made no attempt to hide. "I take it you're pleased with your promotion?"

"Pleased?" she asked, her eyes alight with anticipation. "You have no idea what this opportunity means to me."

An odd expression altered his features, and Sara rose to her feet with a troubled frown. She noticed a curiously smug inflection in the smile he gave her, and there was a victorious edge to his voice as he whispered, "Oh, I think I do, Sara."

Shrugging off her uneasiness, Sara walked to the door in a delighted haze, her mind filled with ambitious plans to prove her worth in an executive capacity. But as she opened the door, she happened to glance back at him. It was then she saw the triumphant expression on his face. With rising fury she realized that once again she had allowed herself to be manipulated.

She had fallen into his hands like a plum ripe for picking, she thought in disgust. One way or another, he was determined to give her the holiday she hadn't wanted to accept from him. She should have remembered Rand wasn't used to being thwarted. Yet, she seriously doubted if foreknowledge would have done her much good. Rand would use any means to get his own way!

For a brief moment she considered retracting her acceptance, but something in Rand's expression warned her not to take the matter further. If she wanted to advance to an administrative capacity under his tutelage, she reasoned, she was going to have to refrain from continually lashing out at him like a child. Openly accusing him of manipulating her to suit his own ends would hurt no one but herself. So she forced back the angry comments seething in her brain and with a façade of civility listened to several belated instructions from him.

Strangely enough, when she finally left his office the only sop to her pride came from the flicker of approval in his steady gaze. But Sara wasn't pleased with such transient satisfaction. The desire to get back at him was strong, and she was determined to give him a taste of the humiliation she was suffering. It was time Rand Emory learned she was in control of her own life, she thought.

Sara attacked the stack of correspondence on her desk with little enthusiasm but a great deal of furious energy. She tried to ignore the nagging little voice in her head that ridiculed her with the truth. If it's really control of your life you want, Sara, the noisy gremlin taunted mercilessly, then why can't you make yourself leave him?

Sara wasn't at all pleased with the answer. She wanted to be near Rand no matter what the circumstances, even if it meant sacrificing her pride. He would never love her, she told herself, but there was always the hope that someday he might want her the way she wanted him. At least then she would have a part of him, she reasoned, if only physically. But she despaired of finding an opportunity to convince him that she was a warm, sensual woman.

But the opportunity to challenge Rand's control came sooner than expected. She was getting ready to leave for home when he strode up to her and placed a handwritten note on her desk. Glancing at the message, her blood rose to a steady boil. "Do you want this delivered tonight?"

Her gaze was fixed on the note with revulsion, but from the corner of her eye she saw him reach into his pocket and extract a small, gaily wrapped box. Placing it by her clenched fist, he said, "I want these delivered tonight."

She reached into her top desk drawer and withdrew a plain envelope and placed the note inside. Carefully sealing the missive, she fought against a sickening sense of despair. When Rand had broken off his relationship with his last mistress, he'd been more than generous with his parting gift. That was over a month ago, and she had hoped . . .

"Shouldn't you take them yourself?" she mumbled, swallowing the bile rising in her throat.

"I have a dinner engagement with Bradshaw in thirty minutes."

Bradshaw was a corporate lawyer new to the Phillips staff. He'd been detained with a court appearance this afternoon and was unable to take part in the final negotiations. Sara guessed Rand wanted to discuss the changes made on the Burroughs contract, but at the moment she didn't really care. Rage was seething inside her, exceeded only by a feeling of betrayal. Her fingers itched to pick up that pretty box and fling it at Rand's head, and only sheer willpower prevented her.

Instead, she clenched her teeth until her jaw ached and frowned up at him. "The delivery boy has gone for the day."

Rand hesitated and finally smiled at her with exaggerated charm. "Can't you drop the note and my gift off on your way home?" His mouth quirked suggestively. "I want to be sure of my welcome when I drop by Corinne's apartment later this evening. I bought her an emerald bracelet to match her eyes. She's the kind of woman who appreciates these small tokens of affection."

I'll just bet she is, Sara thought. She was opening her mouth to tell him to find another gofer when she was struck by sudden inspiration. Her lips clamped together into a strained smile, and she took a deep breath. "I'll be happy to, Rand."

"I knew I could count on you, Sara," he said, a fleeting frown creasing his forehead before he turned and headed for the door. "Tell Corinne I'll be by around nine o'clock. That will give me time to stop by my place to shower and place these contracts in my safe."

She viewed the folders in his hand through the haze of her anger. Not trusting herself to speak, she nodded and watched the door close behind him. Oh, yes, she thought, slowly reaching for the letter intended for his new mistress. I'll make your little delivery, Rand, and I'll personally guarantee the results! Her movements were carefully controlled as she dropped the note into the wastebasket and placed the box in her purse. With a smile of anticipation on her face, she followed Rand out of the office.

5

With a squeal of brakes the cumbersome blue and white bus pulled over to the curb to dismiss its passengers. Fumes from the exhaust belched out a protest as Sara stepped onto the sidewalk, the briskness of her footsteps faltering as she passed the restaurant where her neighbor Patty worked. In a spur-of-the-moment decision, she turned and entered the unpretentious eating establishment. Her mood was effervescent as she followed Patty to a corner booth.

"Can you join me, Pat?"

Patty's gum popped twice before the wad was shifted to enable her to speak. "I'm about due for my dinner break," she replied, eyeing Sara's flushed cheeks. "Give me a minute to speak to my boss, and I'll bring two specials back with me."

"What am I letting myself in for?"

"What do you care?" Patty said, her mouth twisting humorously. "Just eating out should be enough of a novelty to satisfy you. Anyway, we've shared enough meals together for me to know your tastes. Trust me . . . you'll like it."

"Have it your way," Sara retorted good-naturedly, leaning against the padded red leatherette of the booth with a satisfied expression. "But if it's more of that stew you told me was on special a couple of weeks ago, you're footing the bill. I will not eat bunny rabbits!"

"Don't let Richard hear you say that," Patty warned, bending toward Sara confidingly. "According to him, every meal his restaurant serves is a gourmet's delight."

"So it's Richard now, is it?"

Although Patty flushed with embarrassment, she wasn't about to let Sara gain the upper hand with her teasing. With a practiced leer she pivoted gracefully, her rounded hips swiveling in an exaggerated fashion as she moved away. "That man knows quality when he sees it."

And so he should, Sara thought as Patty went to place their orders. Patty had worked for Richard Clark since he first started in the restaurant business, and it was about time he saw her as something more than a capable pair of hands. Sara knew Patty had taken one look at Richard, after meeting him at a party given by mutual friends, and gone off the deep end.

When Patty learned from these same friends that

Richard was looking for someone to help him manage his restaurant as well as to pinch-hit as a waitress occasionally, she lost no time applying for the job. She'd left an excellent position in a prestigious accounting firm to work for Richard, and so far the sacrifice had failed to fulfill Patty's hopes for a closer relationship.

Recently, in an uncharacteristic mood of despair, Patty had confided her love for Richard to Sara. They were sharing a meal together during one of their few mutual free evenings. As they enjoyed after-dinner coffee in Patty's cozy apartment, Sara innocently remarked on her friend's restlessness. Patty stopped her nervous pacing, and, curling up on the end of her couch with a glum expression, she began to talk. With the fair, slightly freckled complexion of a true redhead, the added color in Patty's cheeks as she alternately extolled Richard's virtues and derided him for being a blind, stupid, insensitive fool gave her the look of an enraged Kewpie doll.

"He looks right through me, Sara."

Hearing the hopelessness in Patty's voice, Sara nodded sympathetically. "I know just how you feel," she said. "Men can be a real pain in the . . ."

Sara's marked hesitation had the desired result. Patty's normal ebullience returned as she laughed into Sara's dancing eyes, her own gaze holding friendly curiosity as she remarked, "You sound like a fellow sufferer."

Sara had never experienced a close friendship with a woman her own age. For as long as she could remember her closeness to Sam precluded outside relationships. Knowing his dreams for her, she had taken her schooling seriously and as a result failed to form any but the most casual of friendships. Now, as she found herself sharing her feelings for Rand with Patty, she basked in the warmth of the other woman's sympathetic understanding.

"He sounds as much a pig as Richard," Patty remarked cheerfully.

Before Sara had a chance to either confirm or deny this aspersion on Rand's character, Patty was hurrying into the kitchen. She returned, waving a bottle of brandy in the air. "I'm in the mood to tie one on. How about you?"

That night had firmly cemented their friendship, and although Sara later discovered the true meaning of the word *hangover,* she hadn't regretted the experience. Well, maybe she did have one small regret, she thought wryly. She and Patty had topped off the brandy with conversation, their confidences becoming more intimate as the hour became later. Sara's recollection of what was said was vague, as was the memory of the two of them sneaking down the hall in the middle of the night in search of Freddie. He had been eager to provide them with advice to the lovelorn as well as another brandy, she remembered with a smile, and both she and Patty were still suffering from his teasing.

Sara jumped when a hand was waved in front of her face. "Come back, come back, wherever you are," Patty chanted, depositing herself on the opposite seat with a relieved sigh. "God, my feet are killing me!"

"Serves you right for being a willing victim of slave labor. It's lucky for Mr. Clark you don't get paid by the hour."

"Too true," Patty retorted, a momentary scowl on her face. Then she brightened and settled herself more comfortably in the booth. "But I did get a raise last month. Richard's not penny-pinching, he's just usually oblivious to anything outside of his kitchen."

"Why, Patty," Sara remarked with a smile. "Where's all that Irish temperament . . . all that fine indignation in your voice when you talk about him?"

"Ah, but proving myself indispensable is finally paying off," Patty said, her eyes widening innocently as Sara reacted to the cryptic remark with raised brows.

"What's been happening while I was cramming for exams?"

"Not a thing."

"Patty, are you holding out on me?"

"It's true," the other girl protested, giggling at the disgusted expression on Sara's face. "The last few weeks Richard was as distant as ever, and I just couldn't take it anymore. Tonight I was feeling the strain more than usual, and when he began to point out an error I'd made in the bookkeeping in that cold, patient manner of his, I lost my temper."

At that moment their meal was brought to the table, and Sara's mouth dropped open in surprise as she recognized their waiter. Richard Clark was not a good-looking man. His hair and eyes were a nonde-script brown, his face craggy. He was average in height, with the brawny build of a wrestler. But when he smiled at Sara's obvious discomfiture and she saw the gentle humor in his eyes, she suddenly understood the reason for Patty's unfailing devotion.

Introductions were made, and Sara was once again treated to the warmth of Richard's smile. "So you're the friend Patricia's always going on about. It's about time we met."

"I agree," Sara responded, her eyes twinkling as she noticed she'd lost Richard's attention. He had glanced over at Patty as he greeted Sara, and he seemed to be having the greatest difficulty tearing his eyes away from her friend's vibrant prettiness.

Sara cleared her throat loudly, hiding a smile as both Richard and Patty started guiltily. "I've heard a great deal about you, too, Richard."

He flashed another quick glance at Patty, whose color had deepened at Sara's words. "You have?"

"Patty thinks you're an excellent employer," she said, tempted to laugh aloud at Patty's palpable air of relief. "I understand you'll be opening another restaurant shortly."

The next few minutes were spent in conversation, and soon Richard left to greet new customers. As they watched him walk away, Patty sighed, her heart in her eyes. "Isn't he wonderful?"

"He is rather nice."

"Nice?" Patty squealed indignantly.

This time Sara couldn't suppress her laughter. Finally regaining some measure of control, she gave a rueful shake of her head. "I thought you told me Richard was a pig?"

"Not after what happened tonight," Patty sighed dreamily.

"All right, you've got me dying of curiosity. What happened to put all that color in your cheeks?"

Patty's response was swift and uncannily intuitive. "Only if you promise to tell me why you're celebrating."

"How do you know I'm . . . ?"

"Coming here for dinner isn't enough of an occasion to merit that fighting sparkle in your eyes." Patty laughed, wrinkling her nose at Sara's shocked expression. "You look like that only after you've had a set-to with Rand."

"Am I that transparent?" Sara asked ruefully.

"As clear as glass. Now, do we have a deal or don't we?"

Picking up her fork, Sara cut into the tender filet of lamb on the plate in front of her. As they ate, Patty began to recount her evening in detail, giggling as she described Richard's expression after she had cornered him in his office. "I was tired of being treated like a part of the furniture," she explained, a trace of her earlier anger in her voice.

"You didn't let that Irish temper of yours loose on the poor man?"

"Poor man, nothing." Patty groaned reminiscently. "He let me yell at him for a full five minutes, and then he pulled me into his arms and started kissing me until I thought I'd died and gone to heaven."

"I take it you kissed him back?"

Patty murmured yes, and Sara felt a momentary surge of anxiety. Patty's so vulnerable, she thought, worry creasing a line across her smooth forehead. Was her friend reading too much into the incident? Because of her experiences with Rand, Sara knew it was possible for a kiss to convey little more than a male's natural response to an attractive female. But when she remembered the bemusement on Richard's face when he stared at Patty, some of her anxiety dispersed. He had looked like a man in shock, who was more than ready to begin thinking like a man in love. Yes, she thought in satisfaction, there had been tenderness as well as desire in those brown eyes of his, she was certain of it. How she wished Rand would look at her like that!

As though by telepathy, Patty fixed Sara with an accusing glare. "All right, now it's your turn to sit in the confessional. What trouble have you gotten yourself into now?"

At the word *trouble*, Sara blanched. I must have been out of my mind, she thought, shivering as she remembered some of the words Rand's lady love had flung at her head. That's one message I won't dare repeat, she decided, not at all surprised by a belated feeling of cowardliness. Rand was going to kill her when he arrived at his destination tonight, and she would deserve everything she got. How could she have delivered that bracelet and brazenly informed his lover that their relationship was at an end?

"Sara, surely it couldn't be that bad?" Patty asked in concern.

Sara pushed her plate away, her appetite gone. Leaning her elbow on the table, she cupped her chin in her hand and dolefully returned Patty's scrutiny. "It's much, much worse!"

Quickly, she explained what she had done, not feeling a bit reassured when Patty burst into gales of laughter. "You mean . . . you actually gave . . . Rand's mistress her walking papers?" Patty asked incredulously, hiccoughing between words. "Oh, Sara, you're . . . priceless."

"My hide isn't going to be worth much when Rand catches up with me," she whispered, a horrified expression crossing her features as her mind grappled with possibilities. "How could I have been so stupid, Pat?"

Patty held her breath and swallowed half a glass of water. Putting the glass back on the table, she waited a minute to be sure she'd drowned the last of her hiccoughs. "If you want my opinion," she finally admitted, "I think it was the smartest move you've ever made, Sara. I've always disapproved of the way Rand expected you to field his relationships, and it's about time you stood up to him. Maybe this will teach him a well-deserved lesson."

"Or maybe you'll soon be putting flowers on my grave."

"Oh, don't be silly," Patty protested, her eyes kind

as she tried to reassure Sara. "When you confront Rand, you just remember you had every right to behave as you did. Stand up for yourself, and everything will be fine. I know you're worrying unnecessarily," she concluded, placing a reassuring hand over Sara's clenched fist. "Rand is bound to see the humor in the situation."

Sara returned home buoyed up by her friend's optimism. A long hot shower left her feeling a little more relaxed, and as she prepared for bed she tried to push all thoughts of a certain aggravating man from her mind. By the time she was standing covered from neck to ankles in her favorite granny nightgown, brushing her freshly washed and blow-dried hair in front of the mirror, she had been fairly successful in channeling her thoughts. So when Rand's furious voice accompanied the pounding of his fist on her door, she nearly dropped dead from heart failure.

The moment he entered her apartment, Sara lost all hope of Rand viewing her actions with humor. Her fingers twisted against the handle of the brush she'd forgotten she was holding, her eyes refusing to meet his as he closed the door with a controlled slam that did little to steady her nerves. Swallowing past the lump in her throat, she tried as casually as possible to place a safe distance between them.

But her hour of reckoning was at hand, and Rand swung her around to face him. "Just what," he questioned softly, "did you hope to accomplish?"

Remembering Patty's advice, Sara refused to allow herself to plead for Rand's understanding of what had been, she staunchly convinced herself, no more than an angry impulse. "I'm not certain I know myself."

"Then why don't I take a stab at it?" he whispered, his voice hoarse as he slowly dragged her up against his tense body.

Her senses alive to the warmth emanating from his large frame, she shivered as she realized just how vulnerable she was to him. "Rand, I—"

"That's right," he interrupted, his hands tightening on her slender shoulders. "After what you did, you deserve to squirm, angelface."

"You're the one who should have a guilty conscience," she protested, renewed anger momentarily overriding her caution. "Might I remind you I'm paid to be your secretary, not your procurer?"

"Why, you little . . ."

"Don't act the heavy just because I object to being used as a go-between in your sleazy affairs, Mr. Emory. You're not the only one with pride, and I'm sick and tired of having mine dragged in the dirt every time I'm called on to pacify another of your lovers. Tonight, when you actually had the gall to expect me to deliver your tawdry bribe in person, was the last straw!"

"Don't speak to me of how it feels to be at the end of your tether, honey. Not an hour ago I was greeted by a green-eyed fury who told me never to darken her door again . . . or words to that effect. Actually, her language was more of the dockside variety. Unfortunately, in her righteous indignation the woman failed to throw my tawdry bribe back at me. Emeralds and diamonds," he mused, his voice pained. "Do you have any idea how much your temper has cost me, you interfering little devil?"

"A night in the sack?" she responded pertly, finally scraping together enough courage to look him full in the face.

She immediately wished she'd kept her attention on the front of his shirt. There was an odd gleam in the eyes that held her own, one she was afraid to decipher. It was nearly a look of triumph, but there was also a distinct threat somewhere in there as well. Her mouth dry, she began to struggle against the arms that were slipping around her body.

"If that's all I've lost, then there's a very satisfactory way for you to make amends."

Gasping, she twisted furiously. "You must be out of your mind if you think that I . . ."

"That you what?" he muttered harshly. "That you were jealous at the thought of me sharing another woman's bed and decided to eliminate the competition?"

"I did no such thing!"

His smile was wickedly triumphant. "You've grown up with a vengeance, haven't you? You are now as capable of duplicity as any other woman of my acquaintance, with a slight difference. At least they're honest enough to let a man know what they expect from him in return for their favors."

His disparagement hurt her pride to a degree that shocked her. Anguished, she cried, "Then it's lucky you don't want my favors!"

"Don't I?" he asked silkily. "Then why would I go to so much trouble, not to mention expense, to set you up?"

"You mean you . . . ?"

He nodded. "I've gotten damn frustrated by that distant touch-me-not air you develop whenever I so much as speak to you. For months I've put up with your coldness, and believe me when I tell you that many is the time I've wanted to shake you until your teeth rattled. So I decided to give you something to complain about."

"Are you trying to tell me that the constant parade of women in and out of your office was a sham?" she sneered. "Try another one, Rand."

"I'm a healthy man," he responded dryly. "I'm not going to apologize for normal appetites."

"So who's asking you to?" she snapped.

He shook his head, his smile smugly self-assured. "You do, every time those big black eyes of yours stare at me with disapproval, Sara. So I decided on a plan of action and carefully mapped out my campaign. But I underestimated your stubbornness, and nothing seemed to get to you. This afternoon was a last-ditch effort. I was hoping you'd get mad enough to tell me to go to hell so I could retaliate in kind. God! I was ready to strangle you when you calmly sat there and took your instructions like the perfect secretary. I thought if just once I could make you lose control, I'd be able to break through your shell of indifference."

"Well, you succeeded," she muttered petulantly. "I hope you're satisfied!"

"There's only one thing that will satisfy me now!"

Sara's attention was captured by heated gray eyes, the message in their depths burning a sensual message. When Rand pulled her into his arms, her hand rose in an instinctive gesture of protection. She tried to prevent the lips that pressed against her throat from reaching her mouth. If he kissed her, his triumph would be complete. As it was, his lips burned against the pulse that throbbed uncontrollably against her temple. She might as well have tried to stop Niagara Falls, she thought, the last of her anger slipping away. When his exploring tongue snaked out to taste the corner of her mouth, she was defeated by her own longing.

With a moan her arms went around his neck, her fingers luxuriating in the crisp thickness of his hair as his kisses searched every inch of her face. She was guided by instinct. Arching her back, she pressed herself against the strained material of his slacks and absorbed his responsive groan through every cell in her body. Minutes or maybe hours passed in a sultry haze of pleasure. The neckline of her nightgown was loosened by Rand's deft hands, and her breasts were caressed into tightening peaks. With fumbling fingers she unbuttoned his shirt, wanting the abrasiveness of his body hair against her with desperate hunger.

With a low growl he accommodated her, and no more words were spoken between them. Words didn't matter when the room was filled with soft moans and sighs, and the thundering sound of their accelerating heartbeats. Sara felt Rand's pulse thundering in symphony with her own and knew a sudden, fierce surge of power over the man who held her. She resented the clothing he still wore that restricted the urgency of his movements, and she conveyed her need for a more satisfactory contact by arching her hips in a provocatively innocent appeal. He began to pull away from her.

"Rand, please . . ."

"Oh, God . . . Sara!"

"Make love to me, Rand," she pleaded, her mouth feverish against his taut throat.

"You don't know what you're saying," he gasped, his eyes closing as he swallowed convulsively. "I . . . not like this!"

She clutched at him, her eyes bewildered. "What do you mean?"

"I took advantage of your anger to arouse you."

She relaxed, a complacent smile curving her lips. "Does it matter now?"

"It matters," he echoed hollowly, his eyes tortured as he struggled to control his breathing. "I didn't intend for things to go this far. Do you want to make me despise myself?"

The words were bitterly accusatory, and she flinched in surprise. She gazed at him with wounded eyes and then wrenched herself out of his arms with a force bordering on violence. She straightened the nightgown that hung lopsidedly over one smooth, bare shoulder, and her fingers ached from the force of her grip as she held the material to her throat. "I've been well and truly put in my place, haven't I?" She laughed hollowly. "But don't leave feeling too triumphant, Rand. Maybe I was just trying to see how far you would go with your punishment. It's a pity." She pouted in deliberate provocation. "I was quite enjoying myself!"

"Since I prefer to be up front in my dealings with the fair sex, it's a good thing I stopped." His eyes raked her body with a mocking inspection. "After all, anything grudgingly given isn't worth having, Sara."

Rand strode to the door, slamming it behind him, and for an interminable length of time Sara stood in numbed disbelief. Eventually she managed to cross the room to seek out the comfort of her bed. She drew the blankets close around her shivering form; her eyes stared unseeing into the darkness. The rest of that long, anguished night was spent trying to cope with the cruelty of Rand's actions and the stupidity of her own.

6

Sara stood on an upper floor of the MGM Grand Hotel and grimaced with irritation. The view was well worth studying, she thought impartially. White and pink spun-sugar clouds seemed to hover almost within reach of her hand, while in the distance stood the purple-hazed foothills of the Sierra Nevada. She sighed and cooled her forehead against the thick window glass. When she closed her eyes she was able to evade her own wavering reflection. She had no need to see the despair settling an inanimate mask over her features to know it was there.

Her midnight-black hair was parted in the middle, and the straight, thick strands flowing to her waist only added emphasis to the pallor of the creamy skin stretched too tightly over her prominent cheekbones.

She didn't have to open her eyes to remember the haunted shadows that dulled their obsidian blackness or view the nervous trembling of her body to sense she had almost reached the end of her endurance.

Her lips pursed with determination as she tried to pull herself together. It wasn't like her to be so negative, she realized. But after she had worked herself to a standstill this past week in an attempt to accept the cool distance in Rand's eyes every time he looked at her, her mental state wasn't exactly conducive to positive thinking.

Contrary to her earlier reluctance to attend the Nevada convention, the trip had soon begun to seem like the pot of gold at the end of the rainbow. Rand's motive in sending her as a representative in his place no longer mattered. Several days away from him would give her a chance to come to terms with what had happened between them. She needed time to accept the fact that he didn't, and never would, view her as a desirable woman.

Her expression hardening, she opened her eyes and watched as the clouds drifted across the sky. Pink deepened to crimson on the horizon as the sun began to withdraw its warmth from the day. She caught her breath at the beauty of the sunset only to wonder if any of the people below, still lingering by the olympic-size pool, were as miserable as she was. Sara had learned firsthand over the past few weeks how deceptive the appearance of tranquility could be.

With a moan of distress, she ran shaking fingers

across the black bangs feathering her forehead, shocked by the extent of her cynicism. The four-and-a-half-hour drive from San Francisco had left her feeling sticky and unkempt, yet she couldn't even summon enough energy to bathe. The worried thoughts skittering through her brain precluded activity, and even being surrounded by the sumptuous trappings of wealth wasn't enough of a novelty to put an end to her depression.

Because of her own stupidity, the tension that now existed between her and Rand whenever they were together was rife with the words she should have spoken, the explanations she should have made. But where Rand was concerned, she thought bitterly, she was an emotional coward. Oh, God! She wondered if he despised her more than she despised herself!

Sara raised her fingers to the tightening ache beginning to make itself felt at the top of her spine and arched her neck against her palm. Twisting her head from side to side, she groaned and began to move slowly in the direction of the bedroom. A shimmering crystal wall lamp illuminated her luxurious surroundings, and she frowned as she tried to calculate the expense Rand had incurred by renting an entire suite for the duration of her stay.

True, this wasn't the luxurious Bahamian resort where he had first suggested she go. But she had a hunch that where cost was concerned, these rooms in one of Nevada's most luxurious casino-hotels must run a close second. Heavy turquoise velvet drapes edged lacy sheers as delicate as the gossamer wings of a summer butterfly, while pale blue walls added a touch of classical purity to a long white divan fronted by an elegant glass-topped coffee table.

She scowled and tapped an impatient tattoo against her side with tense fingers. Directly in the middle of the coffee table was a lavish floral arrangement with a note that read, "Forget your injured pride and accept the flowers in the spirit they're given. Eat, drink, be merry, and charge everything to my expense account. See you soon. Yours, Rand."

The man is an enigma, she thought. He mentioned her pride so casually, not realizing how close she had come to destroying what little self-respect she had left. She had wanted his lovemaking so badly, she thought, shivering at the memory of bold hands on her body and a gentle mouth sweeping aside her inhibitions as well as her conscience. For countless blissful moments she had indulged herself in acting out her fantasies until he brought reality crashing down around her head. When she had pushed him away, hurt hadn't been her only motivation. His words to her had made her realize that she couldn't take advantage of a vulnerability that was born of anger rather than need, especially when she was made aware of the contempt he would have felt for himself afterward.

She had never asked for a guardian angel, and because of his own behavior that night Rand had finally been forced to see he could never fit such a role. It was a truth she had known from the beginning.

She had always been too aware of the sensuality in his nature to view him as platonically as he wished, she thought. Sara fought a fresh wave of humiliation.

Oddly enough, considering his experience with women, Rand had been shocked by her reaction to his lovemaking. When she went into work the following Monday morning, he was waiting for her with an apology, his manner hesitant as he tried to discover the extent of the revulsion he thought she must be harboring toward him. She wanted to laugh at his misconception—laugh not at him, but at herself. Her efforts to make it appear that she had gone along with his seduction to punish him had gone sadly awry, she thought. She had never been so stirred by a man, but she had no one to blame but herself. She had been the one who had first become irate and tried to use Rand's angry loss of control to suit her own ends.

She had reveled in her ability to arouse him. Having been privy to the sometimes explicit confidences of several of his lady friends, she had long ago accepted Rand as a highly sexed individual. Unamused laughter rippled from her throat. Rand's master plan had been assured of success from the beginning, though she knew the man's hair would stand on end if he ever discovered how much of his private life had been shared with his seemingly calm, impersonal, efficient secretary.

She knew, for instance, what he liked for breakfast and what he didn't wear to bed. She had also been given a fairly comprehensive impression of his versatility as a lover. Of course, the last she took with a grain of salt. Rand kept himself superbly fit playing handball in the winter and tennis in the summer, but he was no contortionist!

How would Rand be as a lover? A chill feathered her skin as she remembered the look on his face as he bent over her. Self-contempt had been interwoven with a masculine hunger for her body, and his whispered words were proof of the conflicting emotions tearing him in two. She remembered reaching for him with hands that clung, her fingertips caressing as she smoothed the naked shoulders beneath his gaping shirt. His face had been dark with passion, his mouth opening slowly as he lowered his head . . .

God, she had to stop tormenting herself! With an exclamation of disgust, she started toward the bedroom and barely managed to resist sticking her tongue out at the lovely floral arrangement as she left the room. She crossed the threshold into the bedroom and eyed her suitcase with little enthusiasm. It lay sprawled in the middle of a thick burgundy and cream carpet where she had thrown it a few minutes ago, too tired to unpack.

With a sigh of renewed frustration she averted her eyes and looked at the bed that dominated the room. But if she hoped to improve her irritable mood by diverting her attention, she was thwarted by the heavily embossed, cream satin spread billowing over the round mattress. As if the thought of reclining on such a decadent object wasn't bad enough, the bed was on a raised platform, surrounded by a frame from which hung sheer curtains with pale rose swirls overlaying a coordinating cream background.

She uttered an inelegant snort as she noticed the headboard against the cream-colored wall. Braced by shiny gold metal, it was inlaid entirely with mirrors. Suddenly, she saw the luxurious suite as a gesture of Rand's contempt, and her despondency gave way to righteous indignation. The devil had chosen these surroundings knowing very well how much she would hate spending hours alone in a room that positively reeked of sensuality. In his uniquely brilliant manner, he had not only found the most suitable place to stick the knife, she thought murderously, he was also quite capable of twisting it until he drew blood. While she stood here he was most likely enjoying a quiet moment of triumph at her expense.

She could picture his aggravating smile, and she ground her teeth together until her jaw ached. Her first impulse was to head for the reservation desk and demand a more modest room, but that would be playing right into his hands. She wasn't going to give him the satisfaction of suspecting how successful this latest ploy had been. If he called to inquire about the progress of the convention, she was going to gush and enthuse over her accommodations if it killed her, she decided. Shaking her head, her mouth curved into a disgusted grimace. Even with the lights off she was going to feel pretty stupid in a bed that looked like a fluffy white marshmallow!

With a grunt of resignation she gripped the handle of her suitcase and placed it firmly on top of the spread. Releasing the locks, she opened the lid and rummaged around inside for her toilet articles. She withdrew a compact zippered bag containing her brush and comb, makeup, and a toothbrush and reached for her favorite lounging robe. Sitting on the edge of the bed, she lifted the elegant material to her face and inhaled deeply.

She was immediately comforted by the scent of the soft, familiar fabric. A brief smile crossed her face, and she shrugged her shoulders ruefully. The floor-length garment with its long billowing sleeves had been given to her by her father on her eighteenth birthday and was a treasured keepsake infrequently worn. In her present frame of mind, she thought, she needed the security to be found in familiar things. Lifting the robe to her chest, she smoothed the delicate folds with the tips of her fingers. The action triggered a memory of those same fingers tracing a path across the incredible softness of the hair that covered Rand's chest.

With a surge of pain Sara stood and gathered together the items spread out beside her. She was damned if she was going to let Rand Emory spoil the rest of her night! The next few evenings would be taken up with meetings, and she'd promised herself these hours to unwind. Since her shared bathroom at home had only a shower, she was looking forward to submerging herself in a tubful of scented bubbles. She might hate having to spend her free time in this silken love nest, she thought, heading in the direction of the bathroom, but she wasn't going to object to having a real honest-to-goodness bathtub at her disposal!

As she had guessed, the oval tub sunken into the floor was a lure she couldn't resist. She reached out to turn on the light and mistakenly flicked the switch that activated heat lamps built into the walls. Immediately, a vague red glow bathed the room with warmth, and she shivered at its sensual appeal. With an appreciation mixed with guilt she filled the tub with water. She might as well be hung for a sheep as a lamb, she thought as she eyed a box of scented bath crystals provided by the hotel. Reaching out, she sprinkled them into the water with a gesture of bravado.

Sara removed her clothes and lowered herself into the steamy, fragrant bubbles with a moan of delight. Reclining back against the padded headrest, she let cleverly positioned whirlpool jets gradually ease the tension from her body. Languid with pleasure, she yawned and forced open her drooping eyelids. A shocked gasp had her sitting up with a jerk, her head tilted back as she stared at the ceiling in disbelief.

"My God," she muttered incredulously. "Whoever designed this room had definite voyeuristic tendencies!"

Now that her eyes were accustomed to the shadowy light given off by the heat lamps, she glimpsed her nakedness in a ceiling composed entirely of mirrors. A remembered chant from childhood came to mind, and she whispered, "Mirrors, mirrors everywhere. When I see them I stop and stare."

"Who could help it?" she muttered, stepping out of the tub with such suddenness she nearly lost her footing on the slippery cream and gold flecked tile edging the rim. Angrily, she vigorously rubbed a soft towel over her damp skin and pulled on her robe before she reached for the light switch. She knew the red haze now obscuring her vision had nothing to do with artificial heating, and she glared at her own image reflected from the walls as well as from the ceiling. Muttering a curse, she headed for the sink. She brushed her teeth with such ferocity that her gums felt sore when she rinsed her mouth.

She was still mumbling when she slammed the bathroom door closed behind her. After retrieving a novel from her open suitcase, she zipped it closed and dumped it on the floor. She felt as tightly coiled as a spring and knew that unless she found some way to relax she didn't have a chance of getting the sleep she needed. Rand or no Rand, she was getting out of this suite tomorrow! Having made the decision, she felt somewhat better and propped several bolsters against the headboard. At least she had a way of covering these mirrors, she thought as she plopped down on the bed and arranged the brushed velvet folds of her robe around her bare legs.

With a determined flick of her fingers she opened the book. In an amazingly short space of time, considering the state of her nerves, the words began to move swimmingly across the pages. She blinked repeatedly and gradually scooted down until her body rested in a reclining position. Her eyes were closed, and the much-needed sensation of impending sleep replaced the tension in her arms and legs. It might look like a marshmallow, she mused drowsily, but this bed's not at all bad. The framework and draped curtains added an impression of security to her growing contentment, and the mattress didn't sag in the middle as did her sofabed. Her eyes flickered open, and she caught herself smiling in her reflection in the mirrored canopy above her head.

This time there was no shock at her discovery, only a fatalistic resignation. With a disgruntled sigh she rolled over and flicked off the nightstand light, grateful when darkness obliterated her wide-eyed reflection. She had forgotten to put the book down, and now she lay clutching it against her chest while she courted sleep with pleasant thoughts. She would murder Rand! No, that would be too quick. Far better if she locked him in a room made of mirrors . . .

Sara didn't hear the muffled thud as the neglected novel fell to the floor. She was trapped in a funhouse maze, panic on her face as she stared at endless repetitions of her scurrying figure as she tried to find an exit. She couldn't hear the name she called, but a deep masculine voice responded. Turning at the sound, she saw Rand, his hands on his lean hips as he laughed at her predicament. Reaching out, her fingers encountered smooth cold glass instead of the reality of warm flesh. She began to pound against the glass with clenched fists. . . .

Choking back a cry of rage, Sara sat up, trying to

struggle free of her nightmare. She could still hear the sound of her knuckles rapping against the glass, and her head throbbed in the same beat at the memory. With a shaking hand, she reached up to brush aside a tickling strand of hair from her moist temple. As the trapped sensation subsided, she frowned in puzzlement, certain she could still hear the sound of . . .

With a shaky laugh she threw back the covers, at last awake enough to realize that what she was hearing had no place in her dreams. As she slid off the mattress to answer the front door, she chided herself for the vividness of her imagination. She crossed the darkened room carefully and uttered a sigh of relief when she finally reached the sitting-room lamp without injuring herself. That's what I get for putting myself to sleep plotting revenge, she thought. Although it had been an enjoyable diversion, she didn't at all care for the side effects! She swung open the door.

Speak of the devil, she thought, gazing owlishly up at Rand's scowling countenance while both of her hands clutched the door frame. "What are you doing here?"

"Never mind that," he grunted, propelling her with him as he pushed his way into the room. "What in hell do you think you're doing, answering the door without making certain who's on the other side?"

"You're right," she snapped, glaring at him with acute dislike. "If I'd known it was you, I wouldn't have opened it!"

He responded to the taunt with a grin. "Still as

sharp-tongued as ever. I was hoping relaxation would sweeten your temper."

"You've hardly given me time," she retorted. "And that reminds me, just what are you doing here? In case you've forgotten, I was supposed to cover this convention so you could get away."

His smile widened. "I am away."

She wanted to knock those even white teeth down his throat, but instead turned her back and rushed angrily toward the bedroom. "I haven't unpacked yet. I'll just collect my luggage and leave you to enjoy all of this disgusting luxury yourself."

She knew that he had followed her but was still startled when he gripped her shoulders from behind. "You deserve the very best." He increased the pressure of his hands until she leaned against his chest.

"The best way to get back at me, you mean."

"Is that why you think I'd go to the expense of reserving the bridal suite?"

"The bridal suite!"

The exclamation spilled from her tightening throat with a squeak, and she could feel his laughter ripple through her body. Rejecting a tantalizing shiver of response, she forgot her earlier intention to gush and enthuse over his devious choice of rooms. Instead, she whirled to face him with outraged dignity. Even before his arms slid around her waist, she knew she'd made a mistake. Her eyes were perfectly aligned with the silky mat of black hair exposed by the opened neck of his shirt, and, as she watched his chest rise and fall with the rhythm of his breathing, she lost track of what she had intended to say.

With great effort she managed to open her mouth to protest, but to her dismay, the sound that emerged was more in the nature of a whimper. Rand's laughter stopped with a suddenness that increased her self-consciousness to an unbearable degree, and she lifted her head in defiance. But what she saw in his eyes caused a dazed reaction in her no nightmare could ever hope to equal. She began to shake as he drew her closer, his gaze lowering to her parted lips.

"Don't look so panic-stricken," he whispered, an indulgent curve softening the firmness of his mouth. "I didn't say I intended to share the suite with you."

"You didn't tell me you intended showing up here, either."

His lashes flickered down to shade his expression. "That's true."

The prosaic turn their conversation had taken reduced the tension between them, and Sara found the courage to continue questioning him. "Why are you here?"

His answer was flippant. "Would you believe me if I said I missed you?"

"No!"

Although her reply was emphatic, she looked at him doubtfully. She was surprised when he released her suddenly and wandered with studied casualness to the window. Her eyes narrowed in concentration as she stared at his broad back, uneasily aware of an attitude of defeat in his stance. As she moved to stand beside him, his profile was well-defined and rigidly uncommunicative. It was what she'd always thought of as his stone face, only now there appeared to be a hint of vulnerability in the downward curve of his mouth. She was amazed at the impression. Weakness in any form was not something she readily associated with this man.

"Have you finished dissecting me?" he asked lazily.

The question forced her into speaking her thoughts aloud. "I'm sorry, but you seem different somehow."

His laugh held a caustic inflection. "Maybe you're finally seeing me as I really am, Sara."

"Oh, I think I've always been able to interpret your personality correctly, Rand. I'm sure whatever's bothering you will be dealt with in your usual capable manner."

"You're right." He turned to face her, his mouth harshly compressed with determination. "You will be!"

"Me?" Her eyes widened in alarm, her reaction intuitively defensive although her mind told her to proceed with caution. "How like you to try to shift the blame for your foul mood onto me. What's the matter? Afraid I'm getting close enough to see the real man under the suave exterior you like to present to the world?"

"Would you like to, Sara?"

The question hovered between them, enforced by the gravity in Rand's eyes. There was a seriousness in his voice she couldn't ignore, and she wished she hadn't been so eager to taunt him. Not since she was a teenager with an outsize crush had she felt so tongue-tied in his presence, and she couldn't rid herself of the danger signals exploding in her brain. Abruptly, she straightened and shook her head.

"Wouldn't it be easier to tell me the real reason you're here and get it over with?"

"Easier, but a hell of a lot less effective," he muttered cryptically, his mouth firming and losing any trace of vulnerability as he turned away. He walked over to a narrow bar set in the corner of the sitting room and began to rummage around in the portable refrigerator. When he withdrew a pre-mixed bottle of gin and tonic, her breath hissed outward with exasperation. She watched him tear the paper wrappings off two glasses, her impatience reaching explosive proportions.

"Look, I'm not in the mood for any of your protracted game-playing. I'm tired, and I want to go back to bed."

"Have a drink with me first," he suggested, nodding toward the other glass on the bar. "It'll help you unwind."

"I don't want a drink," she remarked, her sulky expression unconsciously provocative.

Rand regarded her for a brief moment before lifting

the drink to his lips. With his other hand he waved in the direction of the bedroom. "Go on to bed then," he said, grimacing as the liquor burned the back of his throat. "But don't forget to pull the covers over your head, Sara."

Her hands were placed firmly against her hips as she scowled at him. "Just what do you mean by that?"

"I thought my words were self-explanatory, but if not, I'll be happy to elaborate."

He put down his empty glass and began to move toward. Reaching out to cradle her face in his hands, he rubbed his thumbs against the underside of her jaw. His head bent, his lips moved against her ear. "When are you going to give in to me, Sara?"

She caught her breath and closed her eyes to savor the delicious sensation caused by his tracing tongue. "I . . . I don't . . ."

"But you do," he murmured softly, "or did I completely misinterpret what happened between us the other night?"

"You're still a-angry with me."

With a husky laugh he nibbled along the sensitive side of her neck. "If this is anger, then may I always exist in a constant state of rage."

Pushing against his chest, she whispered, "Don't tease me, Rand."

The arms that slipped around her waist tightened. "Is that what you think I'm doing?"

With slow deliberation his hands began to move in tantalizing circles against her back. She caught her breath at the swiftness of her response and expelled the trapped air in her lungs when he cupped her buttocks in his palms and lifted her against the cradle of his thighs. Then his hips began to sway in a sinuous dance of arousal, and her eyes widened as her brain registered the hard evidence of his desire for her.

"Does this feel like I'm teasing, Sara?"

7

It feels wonderful, Sara thought. Her arms slowly rose to encircle Rand's neck, and her voice sounded strangled as she gasped a no to his question. His mouth nibbled at her cheeks, her chin, the soft underside of her jaw, and she tilted her head back to allow a further exploration of her throat. "You're ready now, aren't you, sweet Sara?"

"Ready?" she responded vaguely, not really gathering any meaning from his question.

He groaned and brushed aside the collar of her robe. His teeth bit into the soft curve of her shoulder. "Ready to become my woman."

His woman . . . Rand Emory's woman! Just the thought filled her with indescribable joy, and as she gazed up at him her eyes darkened with the strength of her emotions. "More than anything else in this life, I want to belong to you."

"I've waited a long time to hear you say that, honey."

"Aren't you going to return the sentiment and tell me what you want?" she whispered with a smile.

His lips softened in response to her teasing, and he stared at her mouth with undisguised longing. He was pleased with this new, feminine confidence she was showing him, and his reply reflected his thoughts. "I want to be with you in all the ways that matter, little one."

"And those are . . . ?"

His head lowered until his words were spoken against her moistly parted lips. "I want you in my life."

He punctuated his statement with a nibbling kiss against the corner of her mouth. "I want you in my arms."

His hands slid around her back and propelled her against the warmth of his body. "I want you in my bed."

"Will the monstrosity in the other room qualify?"

He responded to her seductive murmur by lifting her in his arms and striding in the direction of the bedroom. "We'll make do with what's available."

Sara linked her hands together at the nape of his neck. "Don't be so sure of yourself, buster," she chided him, her expression smug. "You haven't seen the bed yet."

They crossed the threshold into the other room, and

as they passed the wall switch Sara shifted so she could flick on the overhead lights. She lay back in Rand's arms, laughing softly as she saw the amazement in his eyes as he took in the decor. "My God," he breathed, sitting on the edge of the round mattress with her in his lap. "When I reserved this suite, I had no idea you'd be sleeping in such splendor."

"And here I thought you surrounded me with decadence to drive me crazy!"

With gentle fingers he brushed a strand of hair from her cheek, his other arm supporting her back as he grinned down at her. "Now, why would you think me capable of such deviousness?"

Sara pointed above their heads, her lashes flickering shyly. She heard the gasp reverberate in his chest seconds before his breath was expelled in laughter. "Mmmm, this hotel certainly gives a man value for his money."

"So I was right in my suspicions," she retorted mockingly. "You did hope to share my humble lodgings."

"I know I must appear as guilty as sin, but I didn't plan any of this, babe."

With a single finger she traced the outline of his lips. "I know," she said quietly, "but you will stay with me?"

She looked at him and caught her breath at the longing in his gaze. Her own eyes filled with tears that came from the tenderness spreading outward from her heart for his man. With a choked cry she sought his mouth, and their lips met with a passion they no longer had reason to deny. His hands slipped the silken robe from her shoulders, and when their kiss ended she flushed at the expression on his face.

"The light," she murmured shyly, hiding her face against his chest.

"I want to look at you."

Rand gently laid her back on the bed. As his glance skimmed her body she relaxed, and she grew confident of her own allure as his face showed his arousal. When he rose abruptly to his feet, she stretched languorously against the cool sheets and watched unashamedly as he undressed. Every golden-brown inch of his body was a revelation, and she stared at his powerful physique with wondering curiosity. Sleek, smooth skin stretched over bulging muscle and bone, and her eyes followed the path of softly curling chest hair to where it narrowed to a V. Her own color deepened as she observed the way his stomach muscles tightened as her eyes lowered even farther.

Then Rand stretched out beside her, and she felt filled with rapture as his touch smoothed her skin. Innocence was no barrier to instinct as she arched beneath the mouth that seemed intent on tasting every inch of her and responded to the hands that opened her thighs to his searching fingers. He found what he sought, and she gasped as he gently stroked her to an undreamed of height of stimulation. Her head twisted restlessly against the mattress as she fought to contain the tremors building inside of her.

"Rand, I . . ."

"Don't be embarrassed by the message your body

is giving you, Sara," he pleaded, correctly interpreting the reason for her sudden recoil.

He whispered a muffled endearment against her throat before his head descended. Then his tongue was cooling the heat in her aching breasts with consummate skill. But when his mouth closed over first one tip and then the other, each motion timed to match the languid stroking of his hand, her body answered freely, trying to release the tension he had built up so expertly. Her hips moved of their own accord, shyness forgotten as she surrendered herself to new and unbearably exquisite sensation.

"Please, oh, Rand . . . please . . ."

Sara was plunging into the unknown, the sound of her cries increasing the tightening band of tension in her. With the understanding of a skilled and generous lover, Rand's lips curled in a smile against the soft skin of her stomach. Then, unable to check his own hunger, his mouth sought out the source of her desire. He heard her shocked gasp, but resisted her attempt to close herself to him.

"Look up, Sara," he murmured. "See how beautiful you look to me when you move against my mouth."

With drugged obedience her eyes opened, and in that instant Rand curved his hands around her buttocks and lifted her to him. She cried out, the erotic view reflected by the mirror sending her over the edge into a world of pure sensation. Spasms of delight rippled against the muscles of her stomach until a strong, caressing hand reached up to soothe away the final passionate shudders.

It was the touch of that hand that guided Sara to a deeper level of her body's needs. Now she was the one to hunger for the taste of Rand's flesh, and as she rested by his side she studied the rapid rise and fall of his chest while the blood ran hot through her veins. As though driven by a force inside herself that she barely understood, her tongue began to slide against his throat. With gritted teeth Rand drew in his breath, and her eyes were forced to meet his by the hands that tightened convulsively against her head.

"You don't have to, babe."

Her own whispering sigh matched his in intensity. "Let me, Rand."

In truth, Rand was locked too tightly in the grip of unreleased passion to prevent what followed. Slowly, Sara's mouth savored the taste and texture of his skin. Remembering what he had done to give her pleasure, she licked at his nipples, feeling them harden beneath her tongue. Gently she ran her palms over his arms and chest, and when her hands moved lower his fingers twisted feverishly in her hair.

"Let me love you now, Sara."

The plea was spoken through clenched teeth, and her smile held all the wiles of Eve as she continued her exploration. "You have been loving me."

Encouraged by Rand's responsive groan, her lips circled him briefly and then withdrew. "Look up, darling." She repeated the words he'd spoken to her with confidence, as attuned to his body as she was to her own. "See how beautiful you look to me when you move against my mouth?"

Rand answered her teasing question by carefully flexing his hips, but the convulsive shiver that shook him left him reaching for her with desperate hands. "I can't take much more of that, sweetheart."

Bewildered by the swiftness of their reversed positions, Sara said, "I don't care if you . . ."

His mouth stopped the timid admission in a mutually satisfying manner. Sara clung to him until his head rose, and he murmured, "But I want it all!"

Sara, too, wanted it all. Her hands shifted against the back of his neck, and she brazenly whispered her response against the firm, masculine lips still moist from her tongue. The tenderness of the kiss that followed soon hardened with a depth of emotion that left her gasping. She clutched at Rand's shoulders, and her thighs opened to cradle his hips without a trace of the nervousness she had expected to feel. She was stimulated into an even greater height than before, shocked at how swiftly his hands and mouth could wring a response from flesh sensitized from their earlier encounter.

His frenzy matched her own, yet when he entered her it was with a gentle control that soon soothed the pain of his penetration. Her eyes rose to his face in bemusement, the beauty of his expression at that moment bringing tears to her eyes. Suddenly, he stiffened, his mouth drinking the moisture from her cheeks. "Is the pain bearable, Sara?" he groaned. "Because, God help me, I don't think I can . . ."

He had gone too far to draw back. Her cry of ecstasy when he slid fully into her was misunderstood, the sound stifled by his own moan of remorse. At that instant Sara became a part of Rand, and his anguish became her own. She wanted to accept her share of responsibility for their lovemaking, and now did so gladly.

Lovingly, she soothed his broken murmurs with her mouth and encouraged his quickening thrusts with the welcoming rhythm of her hips. Release came swiftly, startling them with an intensity of feeling that seemed to merge them together into a single, beautiful entity. When it was over, they lay with their arms wrapped tightly around each other. Neither was conscious of the possessiveness implicit in their embrace.

Sara stretched and pulled herself slowly from the depths of the most satisfying sleep she had ever experienced. She was instantly alert and aware of the source of the heat against her back. An amused smile curved her mouth. If her entrepreneur lover could bottle what he'd given her, she thought, he'd be the wealthiest man in the world. She chuckled softly and sighed in complete satisfaction as she continued her speculations.

How the world would change if Rand's magic could be trapped in a capsule! People would be able to throw away their nerve medication, and the word *insomniac* would completely disappear from the dictionary. She wriggled languidly, her memory of the night before refreshed when she felt soreness in her body. It was all Rand's fault, she decided happily. If he hadn't acted with the insatiable stamina of a marathon runner for most of the night, she wouldn't be so aware of the pleasurable aches in her body.

"If you keep that up," a voice still gravelly with sleep protested, "we'll never get to that eleven o'clock meeting on time."

A large, warm hand slid over her naked stomach, and she was pressed back against his muscled thighs. From the effect this maneuver was having on Rand, Sara didn't take his protest seriously. "Mmmm, does it matter?"

"Where has my career-minded secretary gone this morning?"

Reaching back, Sara slid her hand against his hip. Her back arched as she pressed her bottom harder against him. She heard his responsive groan with a contented smile and twisted her head to look at him. "She's alive and well," she assured him with a laugh, "and extremely eager to make a good impression on her boss."

"Shall I fetch your steno pad from your briefcase?" he responded, his gray eyes alight with mischief as he started to roll away from her.

With a squeal Sara pounced, and after a brief tussle Rand lay vanquished beneath her slight but determined body. "Oh, no, you don't," she panted, her dark eyes sparkling with anticipation. "You made me your new assistant, remember? That should give me more influence with my boss than if I were still a mere secretary."

His smile was tender, his gaze lighting with inner fire as he cupped her cheeks and drew her mouth to within an inch of his own. "Is this how you intend to make an impression on me?"

Rand's meaning was blatant, and Sara grinned while settling her hips close to the seat of his desire. "And if it is?" she whispered, tracing his lips with her tongue.

"Then impress me, darling."

He groaned and captured her tongue in his mouth. Then, with capable attention to detail, Rand patiently coached her toward new levels of proficiency.

Rand's prediction was correct, and they were late for the introductory luncheon meeting. They arrived in time for him to give the speech Sara had prepared, and as he addressed the gathering from the podium, she wasn't in the least disappointed in their role reversal. She watched him with pride, impressed with his casual air of confidence as he spoke to his top executives and their wives. Glancing around the room, Sara was convinced that no one suspected that his speech was completely unrehearsed. They listened with rapt attention, their eyes never wavering from the impressive figure he presented.

It was only later, when Rand surprised her by announcing her promotion to executive assistant, that Sara became conscious of the speculation being aimed in her direction. She was aware of a subtle shift in attitude and was made uneasy by the speculative glances she was suddenly receiving from several board members. But she was determined not to allow small minds to destroy the happiness she felt with Rand, and when he returned to his seat beside her she greeted him with a warm smile. His answering grin contained an intimacy no one in the banqueting hall seemed to miss, and Sara told herself she didn't give a damn.

After the meal was finished and the meeting ended, several of the senior members of the board and their wives stopped Sara and Rand before they could make good their escape. More than anything, Sara wanted to be alone with Rand, and responding to their congratulations proved almost more than she could politely stomach. In front of Rand they guarded their words, but Sara wasn't fooled by their surface urbanity. Deep in their eyes was distrust of her suddenly elevated status, if not overt hostility.

Sara couldn't blame them for their suspicion of her, especially when Rand quite openly kept her at his side by placing a confining arm around her waist. By the time they managed to reach the elevators, Sara's neck prickled with the awareness of eyes following their progress across the red-carpeted lobby. She was burning with humiliation, her anger directed at the confident man who seemed not a bit disturbed by the furor he'd created among his staff. What in the world had he been thinking of? she wondered, not trusting herself to utter a word until they reached the privacy of their suite. Once there, she stormed ahead of him into the sitting room, whirling to face him as soon as she heard the door close.

"Rand, how could you?" she cried, her dark eyes following him as he crossed to the bar.

"How could I what?"

She shook her head with exasperation at the casualness of the question and moved to stand beside him. Her teeth ground together in fury when he immediately placed the bar between them. "You know very well what I'm referring to," she said, anger lending her the assurance to ignore his quelling stare.

With a dismissive shrug of his shoulders he withdrew a chilled half bottle of champagne from the portable refrigerator beneath the bar and set two wineglasses in front of her. With deft hands he broke the seal on the bottle, and with a nodding gesture indicated the sterilized wrappings on the wineglasses. "Take care of those, will you, Sara? I'm having the devil's own time with this cork."

She would have refused, but she needed something constructive to do with hands that longed to strangle him. With a muffled exclamation she tore off the wrappings and returned the glasses to the bar with a glare of defiance. To her disgust Rand avoided meeting her eyes, intent only on pouring the champagne. Sara stared at the surfacing bubbles with annoyance, refusing to acknowledge Rand when he returned to stand beside her.

"I did what had to be done sooner or later, Sara."

She shook her head, frustrated by the emotional tears forming in her eyes. "You know what they were thinking, Rand," she whispered, her eyes closing at the memory of knowing smiles leveled at her. "They think I earned that promotion in your bed."

"You and I know that isn't the truth, and that's all that matters," he said. "I decided to take the offensive rather than waiting to be put in a defensive position, Sara. I would have had to announce your promotion eventually, and the same conclusions would have been drawn if I'd waited until the next board meeting."

"They wouldn't have," she argued stubbornly, "if you hadn't made it clear we were staying here together."

Rand drew her into his arms. "Stop growling at me, darling. It's done now, and everything between us will be open and aboveboard. No one will treat you with anything but the respect you deserve, I promise you that."

Sara was unable to resist the particular sweetness of the smile he gave her, and with a groan she rested her head against his chest. "What am I going to do with such an arrogant, opinionated, devious . . ."

His chest rose and fell in a series of rumbling chuckles. "The same thing I'll be doing with a black-eyed termagant for a wife, I imagine."

Wife . . . wife! The word repeated itself in her mind while he captured her open lips with his own. All the desire he had taught her in the dark hours of the night assaulted her in full force at the initial probing of his tongue, and with a moan of arousal she acknowledged his mastery over her senses. Over her senses, but not over her life. As soon as the thought burst into her consciousness, Sara began to resist the urgings of her body. She remembered all the times in the past when Rand had tried to assert his dominance, and she trembled. Was this simply another attempt on his part to control her? she wondered.

Hardening her heart, Sara pulled away from his kiss. Although his arms still held her, she resisted their appeal with all the strength of will at her disposal. "Is this another proposal, Rand?"

He frowned at the sarcastic inflection in her voice, his glance wary as he absorbed her mood. "Do you want it to be?"

Her eyes darkened with the strength of her emotions as she looked at him. "I want to be with you, but . . ."

His lashes lowered to guard his expression. "But . . . ?"

"But I still don't want to marry you, Rand."

His arms dropped to his side, as he remarked tonelessly, "I see."

Although they still stood close to each other, Sara could feel a chasm opening between them. Closing her eyes, she rubbed at her temples in a gesture of frustration. "If you're honest, you'll admit you don't want marriage any more than I do."

"Since it seems I'm not going to be given a choice," he murmured softly, "I'll bow to your superior wisdom."

She glared at him. "Damn it, Rand. What do you expect from me?"

"More to the point, what is it you want from me, Sara?"

"I want you to realize you do have a choice, if you'll only start seeing me as an individual and not just my father's daughter."

She struck her hip with a clenched fist. "Don't you understand? I don't need your protection, Rand. We don't have to feel shame for wanting each other. We can have a satisfying relationship and be together without placing restrictions in our path. I won't be tied down by convention—to marry to satisfy your sense of responsibility toward me. I'm fully adult, able to take care of myself and make my own decisions. Feeling the way I do, marriage would never work."

Sara moved to stand by the window, her back to him as she waited for him to react to her decision. With closed eyes she leaned against the cool plate glass, nausea churning in her stomach as his voice broke the uneasy silence that had fallen between them. "What will work, Sara?"

She shrugged and crossed her arms in front of her chest in a subconscious gesture of defense. "What happens from this point on is between a man and a woman capable of adult decisions. If you want me, I will give myself to you because I choose to do so. Our relationship can only succeed if we share the responsibility for becoming lovers, with respect and consideration shown on both sides. If you can't accept my wishes as those of an equal partner, then tell me now," she said. "Otherwise, our relationship will be pointless. You are a possessive man, Rand. I respect that aspect of your personality, but I won't be pushed into a role I'm not suited for."

"And you think you're suited to be my mistress?" he exclaimed harshly. "You, a girl who was raised like a beloved princess and taught to expect the best life has to offer?"

Her back stiffened as she acknowledged the bitterness caused by his words. "I don't want or need that kind of patronage from you!" she exclaimed.

Sara was glad he couldn't see the sudden vulnerability of her expression as she tried to make him understand her feelings. "Sam sheltered me from any knowledge of our financial status, determined to give me all the things he thought I should have. Because he denied me the right, as his daughter, to share his troubles, he very likely hastened his own death. In the end, no matter how hard he tried to prevent it," she said, her voice trembling with inner anguish, "life's ugly realities touched me, Rand."

"Is that why you're determined to pay the money Sam owed without help from me, because you feel the need to do penance for something that wasn't your fault?"

His approach was muffled by the thick pile of the

carpet, and her body tensed when his hands came to rest on her shoulders. When she shook her head in denial, his fingers tightened. "Why, then?"

"Because I needed a goal to help me find myself," she admitted quietly.

"And now that you've found yourself, Sara?"

"Now I can finally take pride in my own achievements, which is why I won't willingly relinquish my freedom, Rand. I never want to depend on someone else for my strength, the way I depended on Sam. I am Sara Benedict, a person in my own right, and I won't submerge myself in you or anyone else." She drew in a shaky breath, and her voice hardened as she continued. "The decision is yours to make, Rand. Either you take me on my terms, or not at all."

He sounded as shaken as she felt as he replied. "I'll try to make you happy, Sara."

The tension that had kept her muscles locked in anticipation of his rejection dispersed, and with a throaty cry she turned in his arms. "I know you will. Oh, darling," she sighed, slipping her arms around his waist, "I want you so much."

His hands remained on her shoulders, but he didn't attempt to pull her closer. "Sara, before you say any more I would like to apologize for my behavior during the meeting."

"Apologize?"

She stared up at him in surprise, and his mouth twisted in a wry admission of guilt. "I took your acceptance of my proposal for granted, otherwise I would never have placed you in such a position. I was going to squelch any gossip by announcing our engagement at dinner tonight." He hesitated, frowning. "You realize that now I won't be able to protect you the way I'd planned?"

She nodded and traced the scowl lines fanning outward from his mouth with a gentle finger. "I want you, not your protection, Rand."

At last his hands slipped around her back, and he pulled her closer. He rested his cheek against the top of her head. "Enough to live with me, even though it will curtail your freedom a bit?"

"Is that what you want?"

"I don't want a hole-in-the-corner affair, sweet Sara," he sighed, pressing a kiss against her temple. "Not with you."

She tilted her head against his arm and met the tenderness in his eyes with her own. "Then we'll live and love together openly, and to hell with puritanical board members." Her laughter bubbled up from deep in her throat. "They're probably just jealous, anyway!"

"Mmmm," he mumbled against her lips. "They have a right to be."

8

The next several days passed in a whirl of activity for Sara. As far as she was concerned, the Nevada convention was a tremendous success, although the private times spent with Rand tended to color her judgment. Whenever possible they stole away together. The daylight hours were spent sightseeing, as Rand taught her to appreciate the unusual beauty to be found in the rocky desert landscape. Sara knew she would never forget the whistle of the wind as a clump of tumbleweed was blown over the rough, dry terrain, or the almost mystical awe she had felt when the setting sun bathed the Sierra Nevada with vermilion slashes from nature's palette.

The same wonder was repeated in her heart during soft, silken nights spent in her lover's arms. Sara jealously hoarded the memory of those hours, reliving them in her mind whenever her duties as Rand's assistant prevented the physical closeness to him she was beginning to crave with every fiber of her being. She didn't doubt that others were aware of the countless times her eyes searched for Rand in the crowded meeting hall, or that they knew the reason for her preoccupation. But disapproval and conjecture couldn't penetrate the private world she and Rand inhabited. They had donned the armor of love and stood together, protected from the outside world.

When Rand addressed the gathering at the awards dinner, her gaze clung to him, her imagination seeing beyond the superbly cut white dinner jacket to the warm, golden flesh beneath. There was a new awareness in the secretive depths of her eyes, and an unmistakably sensual slant to the mouth that smiled across the room at him with unashamed pleasure.

At the sight of that smile Rand's words halted briefly, and there was a new huskiness in the timbre of his voice when he eventually regained his concentration. But Sara's attention was held by the tenderness she'd glimpsed in his silvery gaze, everything else forgotten as she realized that he, too, was remembering the sweetness of lips that clung together in pleasure, and bodies that seemed incapable of quenching the desire that held them bound to each other.

The awards dinner marked the official end to the convention, and early Friday morning they began the journey home. Sara felt a pang of sadness as Rand drove her car out of the parking lot, but she was too excited about the coming weekend to spare more than a momentary regret for the end of their holiday. She was returning home only to pack and arrange to have her furniture stored, and with any luck her move to Rand's apartment would be finished by Sunday evening. Sara shivered with delight at the prospect. For her it was a dream come true, and as they left the parking lot her eyes were alight with anticipation, her mouth curving into a smile as she contemplated the future.

"You're looking pleased with yourself."

Sara cursed the gear console that divided her from Rand as she turned her head to look at him. "You're looking rather smug yourself."

He laughed softly. "I'm remembering the innovative method you used to wake me this morning. I have every reason to look satisfied."

Sara flushed, extremely relieved when Rand's attention shifted from her to the increased flow of traffic as they merged onto the freeway. Her sensual awakening had been natural, and yet the change in their relationship was too new to entirely preclude shyness. Sara squirmed against the curved leather of her bucket seat, her whole body on fire with embarrassment as she recalled the boldness of her actions that morning.

She had awakened at dawn, and instinctively rolled over in search of Rand's warmth. Not fully awake, her mouth had hungrily wandered over his sleeping form.

It hadn't taken him long to respond. The lovemaking that followed had been gentle and slow and completely fulfilling, and her heartbeat quickened with pleasure at the memory.

A low voice interrupted her heated thoughts. "Mmmm, I wonder what's causing that marvelous color in your cheeks?"

"You know very well," she groaned, all too aware that the color he found so amusing now covered more than her cheeks. Her whole body tingled as she averted her gaze to the passing scenery.

"Sara?"

"What?" Her reply was a short murmur, and his laughter didn't do much to help her regain her composure.

"Are you thinking what I'm thinking?"

"That depends," she said, finally discovering a way to get back at him. With inward trepidation she widened her eyes with feigned innocence and crossed her fingers in hopes he would make the expected response.

Her prayers were answered when his questioning eyes met hers. "On what?"

"On how fond you are of your furniture."

"My furniture!"

"Mmmm, I don't want you to get angry when I throw away your alarm clock."

Sara was absolutely delighted by the confused expression on his face, which swiftly changed to one of comprehension. With restored confidence she leaned as close to him as possible, her eyes holding his as her fingers traveled lightly along his thigh. "From now on I'll wake you up, darling."

"I'll just bet you will," he muttered.

Still looking at him innocently, Sara's hand crept up his thigh. His gasp mingled together with her giggle, and soon their laughter filled the car. Thank goodness they had left before the rush-hour traffic began, she thought. At this particular moment she was fairly certain that Rand's attention wasn't centered on his driving!

They stopped in Auburn to enjoy a leisurely breakfast, and even after spending nearly an hour walking around historic Old Town, it wasn't quite noon when Rand parked her car in front of her apartment building. While he collected her luggage from the trunk, Sara gazed at the place that had represented home to her for so long. As they walked up to her apartment, she realized that although she was excited at the thought of living with Rand, she still felt an aching sadness for all she was leaving behind.

"Having second thoughts?"

Rand's voice was subdued as he entered her apartment and placed her suitcases beside the sofa. With careful deliberation he straightened, his eyes questioning as he searched her face. The gentle inquiry dispelled her mood as she gazed up at him with the warm rush of emotion she felt at his understanding. She murmured a no, and he reached out to pull her within the comforting circle of his arms. Her surroundings abruptly faded away until only Rand held any reality. Her hands tightened around his neck while her mouth eagerly responded to his kiss. Suddenly, Sara felt a surge of confidence flowing like quicksilver through her veins, and with a groan she broke free of the enchantment with which he surrounded her.

"If you expect me to get everything done by Sunday," she said, pressing her cheek against his chest, "then you're going to have to leave. I'll never get any packing done with you here to distract my attention."

"Are you sure you don't want me to stay and help you?"

Some help he'd be, she thought as his mouth moved against the sensitive hollow beneath her ear. She obligingly tilted her head and laughed as she spoke her thoughts aloud. Rand's response was predictable. Her humor bubbled to an abrupt stop as his gaze lingered on her smiling mouth. Sara trembled with anticipation as Rand released her and moved toward the door. She heard the dead bolt click into place, and the blatant hunger that leaped to life in his eyes was an echo of her own. They reached for each other at the same time, with the same need.

The hour that followed was bathed in enchantment as they made love with a desperation they neither questioned nor understood. At the peak of his pleasure Rand shook with emotion against her warmth, his head pillowed against her breast like a child seeking comfort. "I love you, Sara," he whispered brokenly. "I love you so much."

Her own love for Rand was a fervid litany in her

mind, but the words remained unspoken. She cried his name as the last climactic shudder rippled through her body, but she was unable to voice her feelings. To say the words would be tantamount to placing her life and future in Rand's hands, and that was something she couldn't do. She had to remain in control of her own destiny. One day at a time was all she was capable of giving him, and she could only pray that it would be enough to keep their love alive. At the thought her arms tightened convulsively, consciously attempting to keep him a part of her for just a little longer.

Sara prowled restlessly around her office, once again reading the interoffice memo clutched in her hand. She bit her lip in frustration and wondered how long she could endure the pressure being placed on her by the senior members of Rand's staff. With a futile sigh she stilled her restless pacing and dropped into the comfortable leather chair behind her desk.

The subtle persecution had started nearly a week ago, immediately after her return from the Nevada convention. The underlying contempt with which she was being treated worsened after it became known she was living with Rand. The situation couldn't be allowed to continue, she realized sadly.

The adjustments she was having to make in her personal life were difficult enough, without having to endure the added stress of proving her abilities to people who responded to prejudice rather than intellect. She was being judged on a purely personal basis, and the tension was resulting in gossip that was destroying her credibility among even the most junior employees of the Phillips Corporation.

Sara laughed hollowly and crumpled the piece of paper still in her hand. But the date and time written in the upper left hand corner of the missive was seared in her memory, making any hope she might have had for the fulfillment of her career ambitions useless. There was a board meeting being concluded at this very moment, and she hadn't been informed until it was too late for her to attend.

Such petty subversions were becoming commonplace, she thought tiredly, throwing the useless memo into the wastebasket beside her desk. What she was experiencing was job harassment in its most destructive form, and she was helpless to combat an undeclared enemy. No one had openly acknowledged disapproval of her new executive status any more than they would dare to remark upon her personal relationship with their employer.

Instead, they were relying on trivial irritation to gain their objective. She was being made to look like an incompetent fool, and the knowledge caused her to tremble with the helplessness of her position. Eventually Rand would become aware of the dissention within the firm, and she knew him well enough to guess at his reaction. He would champion her cause, and eventually his own credibility would be in question.

Sara winced, her head tilting in a subconscious attitude of pride. Rand Emory was the ultimate power behind the Phillips Corporation, and she knew he could smooth her path with little effort. But that was something she wasn't going to allow to happen, she decided, her eyes hard and determined as she reached for the phone.

The conversation that ensued was with a headhunter, a man paid to find executive staff for a multitude of independent businesses and corporations. On more than one occasion as Rand's secretary she had used this man's services to provide qualified applicants for job openings. His assistance saved a great deal of time and bother, since he was an astute judge of personality as well as qualifications. It was ironic that his help now would put Rand in the position of having to find someone to replace her, she thought, hanging up the phone with a feeling of despondency.

As she slipped a blank piece of paper into her typewriter, Sara only hoped she could make Rand understand her reasons for the decision she had just made. But her hope was in vain, as she learned within minutes of stepping into his office. He wasn't in the best humor to begin with, and she knew she would have to tread lightly if she hoped to come out of this confrontation with her dignity intact.

"Where the hell were you?" he barked, a scowl drawing his brows together in a dark line. "I held off starting the meeting as long as I could, and felt like an idiot when you didn't show."

"It won't happen again," she promised, slowly reaching out and handing him her typed resignation.

She quailed at the expression of disbelief on his face but remained firm in her decision as he questioned her reasons for wanting to leave his employ. She knew better than to tell him the truth, which weakened her explanation considerably. Eventually, she was left with no recourse but to appeal to him on a personal level.

"Rand, I'm sorry if you feel I'm letting you down, but I find it impossible to be both lover and employee."

He leaned back in his chair, his features cast in defeat. "I was afraid of this, honey."

She smiled and bent forward to brush his hair off his forehead. "It's not the end of the world, Mr. Emory. We'll still have our evenings together."

Rand pulled her onto his lap, ignoring her when she nervously reminded him that someone might walk in on them. "If we were married, you wouldn't worry about being found in my arms."

"But we're not," she responded. Her tone was stilted, and she avoided his eyes.

"Sara, I don't want to lose you," he muttered, pulling her down until her body was curled against his chest. "I know Bates and Fitzgerald have been giving you a hard time. It's just a pity their sanctimonious posturings have affected the rest of the staff."

She looked at him in surprise. "You know what's been going on?"

He nodded, his expression grim. "But eventually this whole situation will blow over and things will return to normal."

"I don't think so, Rand."

"You knew what to expect from the beginning, Sara."

"Knowing what to expect isn't the same as living with the results," she remarked quietly.

"And do you imagine avoiding a board meeting is the best way to prove your worth to the firm?"

The gentle rebuke in his low tones was more than she could stand, and she glared at him while hurt vied with indignation in her eyes. "Don't you know me better than to think that I . . ."

Her words faltered to a halt as Sara realized what she had inadvertently admitted. Rand's expression sharpened, his body tensing as he stated, "You didn't know the damn meeting had been scheduled, did you?"

She shook her head and his arms tightened in anger. "Damn, if they weren't contemporaries of my grandfather's, I'd force them into retirement before they had time to spread any more of their maliciousness."

"My way is best, Rand."

As an attempt to soothe his ire, her calmly voiced statement fell sadly short of the mark. "Like hell it is," he said, reaching past her to crumple her resignation in his hand.

With a muttered curse it was thrown across the room, the balled paper hitting the door before bouncing onto the carpet. Sara watched its progress, and her lips curled in amusement. She chanced a glance up at him from beneath her lashes. He looked as if he'd just found a bug in his milk, and she couldn't stop herself from laughing out loud. His lips twitched, and soon his laughter joined hers.

"Are you certain you want to do this?"

Her mouth firmed resolutely. "I'm sure, darling."

"What am I going to do without you around to bully me, woman?"

Her lashes fluttered seductively as she traced his mouth with her finger. "That's the good part," she whispered, sensing the one certain way to shift his mood. "You'll be all the more eager to come home to me if I'm not pushing you around all day."

He reacted to the promise in her eyes by jumping to his feet and pulling her with him. "Home sounds pretty good right now. I'm tired and should get to bed as soon as possible."

"At six o'clock?"

His gaze roamed from the top of her head to the tips of her feet, and she saw a distinctive gleam in his eyes as he caught her arm and began a pushing maneuver of his own. "The sooner the better!"

Sara received his muttered exclamation with matching eagerness and a very definite sense of satisfaction. She had just joined the ranks of the unemployed, but somehow going home with Rand eased the ache in her heart. They stepped into her office to collect her purse and coat, and she didn't look back as they headed for the elevator. Although she would return to give proper notice and train someone else to take her place, her thoughts were already jumping ahead to the future.

Sara was suddenly excited at the prospect of the new challenges she would be facing in the coming months, and the knowledge strengthened her belief in the rightness of her decision to leave the Phillips Corporation. She and Rand needed to concentrate on each other without being influenced by their working relationship, she could see that now. In a burst of awareness she glanced up at the man who walked by her side. There would be other career opportunities, she thought, but there could never be another Rand in her life.

During the drive home Rand remained unusually quiet, his brow creased in a frown of concentration. The day had taken its toll on Sara's emotions, and she was almost grateful for his preoccupation. But that was before she learned the reason for his abstracted air. Her awakening came after they had eaten a simple meal of soup and sandwiches and retired to the living room with their coffee.

She was stirring cream into her cup when Rand reached for his own and settled down beside her on the sofa. She heard him sigh as he leaned back, and a small smile curved her lips at this betraying sound of contentment. Slanting him a sideways glance while pure mischief glinted in her eyes, she murmured, "You certainly had me fooled, Mr. Emory."

Rand's cup remained suspended in midair while he gazed at her over its rim, his confusion evident in his expression. "I beg your pardon?"

"You rushed me home with the sole intention of watching me slave over a hot stove." With studied deliberation Sara replaced her cup and saucer on the glass table in front of the couch and emitted a loud groan. "It's humiliating when all a woman gets for her sexy thoughts is dishpan hands."

Rand's own cup was plunked onto the table with a rapidity she admired. Although she did spare a wincing thought for the delicate china, her attention was fully captured by Rand when he pulled her onto his lap. Her fingers eagerly buried themselves in the crisp hair at the nape of his neck, and when his laughter continued a little too long her teeth nipped sharply at the cleft in his chin in retaliation.

He sucked in his breath and buried his mouth against her neck. There he bit his way along the sensitive cord and worked his way upward until he had paid equal attention to the lobe of her ear. Sara shivered. "That's much better," she murmured.

"I was only thinking of you, my darling."

"Is that so?"

"Mmmm," he said softly, his tongue tracing the curve of her jawline with great attention to detail. "A gentleman never ravishes a lady when she's hungry."

Sara stretched with feline satisfaction. "That's a contradiction in terms," she responded huskily. "Surely a gentleman should find out what his lady is hungry for before reaching such a decision."

His eyes darkened, and his mouth curved sensually as he whispered, "You're asking for it."

Her own laughter erupted, and her hands slid around his neck until she cupped the sides of his face. "Now you're getting the message, hotshot."

His kiss was hard, brief, but tremendously satisfying. When he again lifted his head they were both breathing heavily, and Sara was stunned by the rapidity of her arousal. Burying her face against the front of his shirt, she murmured unintelligible words. Her embarrassment grew when he chuckled delightedly, and he tightened his arms until the hardened tips of her breasts were resting against his chest.

"Oh, Sara," he whispered, his mouth moving hotly against her throat. "You are such a delight . . . such a joy to me."

"I . . . I'm glad you can still think of me that way, especially after today."

"Now that I've had time to get over the shock, I realize you were right to hand in your resignation, Sara. There's no reason for you to go on working, and God knows you've earned a rest."

Sara felt a chill feather her body at his words. Rand actually thought she didn't intend to find another job. What in the world had she said to give him such an idea? she wondered. She thought back to their conversation in his office and drew a startled breath. They had discussed her reasons for leaving, but no matter how hard she tried, she couldn't remember mentioning her plans to secure another position. She hadn't thought it necessary to go into details, she realized. She had expected Rand to remember her obligation to pay off her father's debts and had simply taken his understanding of her need to work for granted. They had both formed erroneous assumptions, she thought sadly, as they had so often done in the past.

Strengthening her resolve, Sara began to protest against his misapprehension. "Rand, I don't think you understand . . ."

Deaf to her halting protest, Rand continued speaking as though she'd never interrupted his train of thought. "It's about time I took some time off myself, honey. I'm afraid I can't delay my trip to Los Angeles, but while I'm gone you can interview someone to take your place. When I get back I'll delegate responsibility for a change, and we can escape to the Bahamas for a month. Would you like that, sweet Sara?"

Swallowing with difficulty, Sara stared into eyes sparkling with boyish excitement. This was a side of Rand she'd never before encountered, and no matter how hard she tried to find the words, she couldn't bring herself to destroy his enthusiasm. She was trapped by her knowledge of how seldom he relaxed, and concern for him rapidly diminished the urgency she felt to correct his thinking. It would probably be months before she found a suitable position, she thought, and for Rand's sake she wasn't going to borrow trouble.

She could give him today, and hopefully several tomorrows. With a sigh she buried her face against the hollow at the base of his throat and breathed in his scent with a quiver of pleasure. Surely getting Rand to unwind was reason enough to delay a confrontation, she argued guiltily with her conscience. With tenderness she traced his features, and soon the opportunity to speak was lost beneath the fervent warmth of his mouth.

One day at a time, she thought as Rand lifted her in his arms and carried her into the bedroom. His smile as he joined her on the bed blanketed the weakening voice of her conscience. I'll explain everything tomorrow, she vowed silently, her body beginning to respond with tingling joy to the touch of his hands. Tomorrow . . . !

9

The old proverb "Don't put off till tomorrow what you can do today" didn't apply in Sara's case. She never seemed to find a suitable opportunity that weekend to discuss her plans to find another job, and by the time Rand left on Monday for Los Angeles she felt guilty but relieved. Taking advantage of the reprieve, she stopped herself from worrying about the inevitable confrontation with Rand by finishing up at work and finding a suitable person to take over her position. There didn't seem to be enough hours in the day to accomplish the tasks she'd set herself, and her nights were spent in a merciful fog of exhaustion.

But eventually two weeks passed, and there was no reason to delay her departure from the Phillips Corporation. Every loose end had been efficiently tied, and

Rand's new secretary was trained and prepared to handle any last-minute problems that might arise in Rand's absence. Sara knew he would be pleased with Mrs. Gerard, just as she knew how proud he'd be of her if he knew how capably she'd dealt with the hostility and annoying interference of the rest of his staff.

Even though it was common knowledge that she had given her notice, they had still made sure Mrs. Gerard was told all the latest gossip. To Sara's relief, that capable lady only sniffed with disdain and turned a deaf ear to their maliciousness. If anything, Sara thought, the respect and consideration with which Maggie Gerard treated her seemed to increase.

When her last day at work finally arrived without Rand having returned, Sara felt hurt and lonely when she walked out of the building for the final time. Unable to stand the thought of returning to an empty apartment, she drove across town to visit Bob and Edith. As had happened when Sam died, she suddenly needed the loving companionship of her old friends.

The Hastingses greeted her with all the enthusiasm she could have wished, but Sara's depression didn't lighten. No matter how hard she tried, she couldn't seem to shake off an urge to burst into tears. Of course, Edith's sharp eyes noticed her preoccupation, and after Bob left the house to buy some of his favorite pipe tobacco Sara knew she was in for a lecture. Her uneasiness was justified. Bob hadn't been gone two minutes when an unusually flustered Edith began to speak, the light of battle in her eyes.

Although Sara had tried to forestall the confrontation by jumping to her feet and mumbling something about the lateness of the hour, Edith got right to the point. Shaking her head until the tightly permed gray curls bobbed, she said, "I know it's none of my business, but I've always been one to speak my mind, Sara. Bob and I are shocked at Rand's behavior. You're just a young girl with a head full of nonsensical dreams, but he's a grown man whom we always trusted to do what was best for you."

Sara sighed her exasperation at Edith's condemnation. "I gather you both disapprove of our recent living arrangements?"

Edith's mouth firmed, and she wagged an admonishing finger in Sara's face with the confidence of a woman who believes in honesty between herself and the people she loves. "I don't approve of these modern goings-on, and neither does Bob. You and Rand should settle down proper, and you know it!"

Sara repressed the irritation she felt at the rebuke and responded to her friend's disapproval with a distant expression. "Our relationship suits us fine, Edith. I know you and Bob worry about me, but I'm not a little girl anymore. I know what I want, and it's not a place at Rand's feet. I wouldn't be any good at fetching his pipe and slippers."

"Humph, there is such a thing as compromise," the elderly woman snorted as she accompanied Sara to the front door. "I just don't understand you, girl. Sam would turn over in his grave if he knew the way you were carrying on."

Sara's gaze hardened. "Let's leave Sam out of this, Edith."

Knowing she'd gone too far, Edith's face crumpled in remorse when she saw the pain in Sara's eyes. "I don't know what to make of you anymore, Sara. I know I'm an interfering old woman, but it hurts me to see you doing this to yourself. Brittle sophistication might suit some, but you've always been a tender-hearted child. Since Sam's death you've tried to hide your loving heart, but sooner or later you're going to realize that playing games with Rand's emotions is going to irreparably damage the love he feels for you."

"Rand and I understand each other, Edith," Sara said, smiling reassuringly.

"And do you also respect each other?"

"Of course I respect Rand," Sara gasped, indignation now rife in her voice as she sought to protect Rand's image in Edith's eyes. "Your faith in him wasn't misplaced, Edith. He asked me to marry him, but I refused!"

"Why in the world did you turn him down when you love him so much?"

"Because I do love him, Edith," she replied. "Rand wanted to do the right thing because I'm Sam's daughter, and I won't let him sacrifice his freedom for his principles. Our present arrangement satisfies both of us, it really does." Sara reached over to Edith and whispered, "Please, don't worry about me. Rand and I are happy the way things are."

Edith shook her head, her expression heavy with sadness. "I thought you knew Rand, Sara."

"What do you mean?"

"I think you'll discover that for yourself soon enough, honey."

Edith's cryptic remark stayed in Sara's mind as she drove home. By the time she let herself into the penthouse apartment she shared with Rand, Sara felt the throbbing behind her eyes escalating into a severe headache. The sudden shrill ringing of the phone did nothing to alleviate the condition of her head, and she rushed to answer it before its piercing summons had a chance to do further damage.

"Sara, I've been trying to reach you for hours."

The voice belonged to Christopher Allen, the man she'd hired to find her another job. With a rapidly drying mouth she said, "I'm sorry, Chris. Do you have some news for me?"

Mollified by her apology, the man's voice rose several decibels as he nearly deafened her with his enthusiasm. Sara winced, her pulse accelerating as she listened to him outlining the position he'd found for her. "Your interview is set up for tomorrow morning at nine. You'll be meeting with Richard Langley, the top honcho himself. The man likes the people who work for him to project self-confidence, Sara. You just keep in mind that your qualifications are just what he's looking for, and you'll come through the interview with flying colors."

"Thanks for the vote of confidence, Chris."

A fleeting thought of Rand tempered her own excitement at the possibility of going to work for one of the most well-known financial investment firms in the country. After praising Chris for a job well done, Sara hung up the phone and went into the bathroom. Once there, she began to search the medicine cabinet for aspirin. As she swallowed the tablets she tried to imagine Rand's reaction if she were hired. She took it for granted that the president of Langley and Associates would want her to start work immediately. Which would mean the trip to the Bahamas would have to be canceled, she thought, viewing her bleak expression in the mirror above the sink.

Rand would just have to understand what this opportunity meant to her. She knew he was looking forward to their proposed trip, and although she hated to disappoint him she had long ago decided where her priorities lay. As she'd told Edith, she wasn't the pipe-and-slippers type of woman. Furthering her career was extremely important to her if she hoped to realize her ambitions. Once again she glanced at her reflection in the mirror and winced at the discontent marring the soft curve of her mouth. With a muffled expletive she filled her water glass again and drank thirstily.

Sara found the silence surrounding her oppressive, and with a frown she stripped off her clothes and stepped into the shower. The cool flow of water over her body was welcome, but she felt too claustrophobic to linger long in the glass-enclosed stall. Using a lilac-scented soap, she hurriedly lathered and rinsed her body. The herbal shampoo was next, and a small grin curved her mouth as she sniffed the steamy air with real pleasure.

She smelled like a garden. It's a pity Rand's not here to enjoy the results, she decided. Her smile disappeared, as did her momentary enjoyment. She missed him so badly, and that frightened her. She couldn't let herself become dependent on him, especially since they were now living together. She sighed and shook her head. It wasn't supposed to be like this, she thought tiredly.

The last of the shampoo disappeared down the drain, leaving her hair squeaky clean. After turning off the taps, Sara stepped out of the shower and wrapped herself in a large towel. She tucked the ends firmly between her breasts and walked into the dressing room. She used a brush and a blow dryer on her hair with vicious thoroughness.

God! she thought. Rand had been gone for two weeks, and it seemed more like a year. With the towel still around her, she set her clock-radio for seven before flopping down tiredly on top of the bed. As she stared at the ceiling with blank eyes, her mouth tightened in frustration. Should she fly to Los Angeles after her interview to be with Rand? It would give them the rest of the weekend together, and if she got the job, there would be an advantage in breaking the news to him in impersonal surroundings.

Who am I trying to kid? she thought, scraping her lower lip with her teeth. She was making up excuses for going to Rand because she missed him unbearably, and she wasn't happy at the discovery of her own weakness. With a disgusted murmur she closed her eyes, relieved when the pounding in her head eased to a tolerable ache. The day's tension began to melt into immediate lethargy as she gave herself up to sleep with a grateful sigh.

Sara wasn't aware of how much time had passed when she felt the delicious heat of another body. She murmured drowsily and pressed her back against Rand. Her movements were languorous when she stretched, and she arched her breasts against his eagerly searching hands. "I'm glad you're home," she whispered.

She smiled when she realized she no longer wore her towel and pressed against a pair of hard, naked thighs in silent encouragement. Rand's gasp sounded against the back of her neck, his mouth hungry against her flesh. Her response was immediate, and her leg shifted over his hip as she accommodated herself to his thrusting hardness.

"God, I missed you, babe!"

"It feels like it," she agreed huskily.

Without changing their positions he entered her and laughed softly when she gasped with pleasure. "Did you miss me, honey?"

Sara moaned, the days without him escalating her response to his teasingly slow thrusts. With a muted cry she increased the undulation of her hips, her body convulsing almost immediately with release. But Rand wasn't finished with her. Again and again he held himself in rigid control while he brought her to repeated climax. It was only when she thought she would die with pleasure that he uttered a shuddering cry and found his own satisfaction.

With a lusty sigh he lay back and drew her into his arms. Twisting his head on the pillow they shared, he shot her a smug grin. "I guess you did miss me a little after all!"

"Don't look so pleased with yourself, Rand Emory," she retorted with an answering smile. "You just caught me with my guard down."

"I wish I could," he replied cryptically, a strange expression on his face.

He soothed the puzzled frown from her brow with his lips, and Sara drifted once again into a contented sleep. But for a long time Rand resisted the rest his body craved. His arms tightened around the woman he held, desperation adding despair to his thoughts.

Sara reached over groggily to stop the shrilling alarm and lay for a moment trying to wake up completely. Rand's large, warm hand had shifted from her stomach to her hip, the sound of his breathing an indication that he still slept. With exaggerated care she began to edge off the mattress, her toes curling into the rug as she straightened to sit on the edge of the bed.

"Where do you think you're going?"

The teasing voice was accompanied by a lunging body, and Sara squealed a protest as she was forcefully propelled onto her back. She gazed into

Rand's gray eyes with assumed indignation, but her voice held laughter as she said, "You almost caused me to have a heart attack!"

"Then we're even," he mumbled against her throat. "After that marathon last night, it's a wonder my old ticker's still functioning."

Sara gasped as his kiss wandered to her breast, shivers rising on her skin as his lips began to pull gently on her nipple. "Remember your heart condition!"

Contrary to her words, her hands clasped the back of his head to keep him right where he was. He laughed and licked at her with an impudent tongue. "Just be gentle, and I'll manage somehow."

"I can't be gentle," she groaned, arching her back to indicate the depth of her need.

"Then let's take our chances," he whispered, his hand replacing his lips while his mouth wandered across her stomach.

"But I have to get up," Sara wailed.

"I thought that was my job."

Her cry turned into laughter, until Rand parted her thighs. Then all thoughts but those of him left her mind, and she responded to the touch of his mouth against her aching warmth with an urgency that shocked her. Higher and higher he took her, until she cried aloud with her pleasure. Her hands clutched at his shoulders, drawing him up until he filled her with his passion. Then it was his voice she heard, gasping words of need and desire in a litany of love that burned through her, warming her heart as he slumped in her arms.

No matter how many times they came together, she realized in wonder, their hunger for each other only seemed to grow stronger. With hands that shook she smoothed the black hair on his chest, and she snuggled against his side with a little purr of satisfaction. For what seemed ages they lay together, until Sara's gaze fell on the digital numbers of the clock. With an exclamation of disbelief she jumped out of the bed, hearing Rand's voice calling to her as she disappeared into the bathroom.

She was turning on the shower when Rand appeared in the doorway. "What's your hurry?"

She met his impatience with a good measure of her own and blurted out her news without a smattering of the diplomacy she'd planned for so long. "I've got an interview at nine this morning."

"A job interview?"

Rand's question was spoken quietly, but Sara was aware of the anger beneath the surface of his words. Avoiding his eyes, she wrapped a bath towel around her body, suddenly conscious of her nakedness. "Yes, it's a job interview, Rand."

With a courageous gesture she was far from feeling, Sara tilted her chin at a defiant angle. "I never promised to stop working," she said, shivering as she met the curiously blank expression in his eyes. "You made the assumption on your own."

"And you simply let me go ahead and make plans for us when you had no intention of giving me a little of your precious time."

"That's not fair," she said, her anger growing at his

unreasonable attitude. "I was certain Chris would take a little longer in finding me a job. I meant to tell you he was looking for a position for me, but you started making plans for us. By that time I just didn't know how to explain without appearing indifferent to your happiness."

"I'm sorry I placed you in such an awkward position, Sara. You explained the rules of our relationship from the beginning, and it's not your fault I forgot the way the game was supposed to be played."

"Sarcasm isn't going to help this situation!"

"No, you're right," he exclaimed, running his hand through his hair in a distracted manner. "But a little honesty between us would help our relationship in the future. That is, if you give a damn about a future together."

"You know I care," she retorted, her eyes flashing angrily. "But do I have to give up all the plans I've made for my life before you're satisfied that I care enough?"

"Now who's being sarcastic, Sara?"

Sara struggled to regain control of her emotions by holding her breath and inwardly counting to ten. When she was certain her voice wouldn't betray the pain she felt at Rand's callous accusations, she replied to his taunt with what dignity she had left. "Please, Rand," she said, turning a dismissing shoulder to him as she took her watch from her wrist and placed it on the tile counter. "I'm running late enough as it is. Would you please leave so I can get ready?"

He did as she asked, but not before she saw his

expression harden with anger. Closing the shower door, she winced at her behavior. She could imagine how he felt, finding out her secret so soon after their lovemaking. But it was nearly eight o'clock, and she didn't have time for lengthy explanations. If she didn't leave in the next twenty minutes, she could kiss that job Chris had found for her good-bye. She would mollify Rand after she returned home, she thought, turning off the water and drying hurriedly. It would take her fifteen minutes to blow-dry her hair and put on her makeup, so there was still a chance for her to make the interview on time. Suddenly, she realized just how badly she wanted this job. Soothing Rand's ruffled feelings would have to wait until later!

But during the days that followed, Sara forgot all of her good intentions. She became fascinated with training for her new job, and the hours she put in at the office were grueling. Each night she practically collapsed from exhaustion, often not making it home for dinner. Rand became used to receiving abrupt explanations over the phone just as he became used to the work Sara brought home every weekend. He never complained of her preoccupation since he himself seemed to be spending more and more time at the office. In a way, Sara found his return to his previous workaholic pattern a relief, especially on the days that Langley and Associates held their board meetings.

It was during such a meeting that she found herself considering the irony of the shift in her career. She left the smoke-filled boardroom and walked down the hall toward her office, her thoughts centered on memories of her father. That Sara Benedict, daughter of a man who died burdened with mountainous debts due to unwise stock speculation, was now in the position of advising others on the safest and most profitable ways to invest their money, seemed a cruel quirk of fate. What she wouldn't have given, she thought painfully, to have had this expertise when Sam was alive!

But wanting to change the past did no one any good, she reminded herself. At least through careful investing of her own excellent salary she would soon have the satisfaction of knowing she had cleared her father's name. Each newly learned facet of her profession brought her closer to her goal, and she was grateful for the opportunity to learn. She didn't begrudge the hours she worked any more than she had when she was getting her college degree. She knew she thrived on challenge, and she eagerly threw herself into her work with single-minded attention to detail.

Sara returned the casual greetings of several of the staff who stood waiting for the elevator but declined their invitation to join them at Jack London Square for their usual Friday-night revelries. Spirits generally ran high as the weekend approached, and a great deal of career stress found an outlet inside the Overland Saloon, a popular bar reminiscent of early San Francisco history. Her refusal was met with good-humored teasing and a couple of enthusiastic slaps on the back, and with a departing wave of her hand Sara continued on toward her office.

She had accompanied her co-workers to the Overland on several occasions, often enough to avoid earning a reputation as a goody-two-shoes, or worse yet, a woman who thought herself better than they because of her relationship with Rand Emory. She had met their initial suspicion with poise and dignity, anticipating the prejudice her position as Rand's mistress would bring her way. Luckily, when all but the most sensation-seeking of her colleagues accepted her relationship with the president of the Phillips Corporation as old news, Sara ceased to be a current item of office gossip.

She was triumphant at the knowledge of their acceptance of her as an individual, and basked in the warmth of a camaraderie she had never known before. She belonged to a group that boasted some of the brightest young executives in San Francisco's financial district, she thought with pride, and her acceptance into the inner circle was entirely due to her own efforts.

From the start, she knew it was important to win their friendship. Often after working late she accompanied her co-workers for a meal at one of the city's choicest restaurants, and later they usually ended up across the bay at the Overland. There they toasted everything from market fluctuation to her secretary's new baby, and one night, when she had eagerly led the cheering as one of the mustachioed waiters jumped onto the long bar to belt out an Irish lullaby in a pure tenor voice, they had toasted her as well.

She had won acceptance by her peers without being accused of sleeping her way to the top, but at what cost? She felt her mouth tighten with a tension that was becoming all too familiar when she thought of Rand, and she sighed defeatedly. She and Rand seemed to be further apart than ever, she thought, especially since she had ignored his protests and returned to work. Although he had eventually accepted her reasons for striking out on a career of her own, understanding of her motives hadn't lessened his antagonism. Lately, she sensed an undercurrent of reserve in his manner toward her, which she attributed to the growing amount of time they spent apart.

During the past few weeks the evenings they managed to spend at home together seemed to end with them arguing, and more than ever she regretted the necessity of resigning as Rand's assistant. If she had remained with the Phillips Corporation and continued as his executive assistant, she thought, they would at least have spent more time together. As it was, she was beginning to feel guilty at the distance growing between them. She felt as though Rand were blaming her, and it just wasn't fair. Leaving his firm had been necessary if she hoped to retain her pride—he knew that as well as she did. Anyway, she thought bitterly, Rand wasn't entirely blameless for time spent apart. He no longer made much of an effort to adjust his schedule to accommodate her own as he had when she'd first started working. If anything, she sometimes got the impression he was going out of his way to avoid her.

Sara passed the receptionist's station with flagging energy and entered the sanctuary she'd earned for herself. The large room with its plate-glass window at one end had been professionally designed to combine the more functional aspects of an office with luxurious comfort. She passed a pair of modular white leather chairs, the recessed lighting overhead catching the sheen of golden bronze in the curved framework. Her desk was also braced with sculpted bronze topped by smoked glass.

Hardly practical, she thought, her mouth twisting wryly as she passed by the desk and stepped into an adjoining alcove that hid such mundane things as ugly gray files and shelves containing the necessary equipment used to run a business enterprise. But as long as her clients were impressed with the original prints on the white walls and the thick, steel-blue carpet their designer-shod feet crossed to reach her desk, she put up with the inconvenience.

If only, she thought, Rand was as impressed with the success she was making of her new career. Then they might be able to talk together without her being afraid of mentioning her work. She laughed under her breath, the sound bitter. It sometimes seemed that both she and Rand had become afraid to talk to each other. To communicate would be dangerous, she thought, since they might say something they would live to regret. She paused as she donned her coat, a confused frown curving her brow. God! When was the last time she and Rand had made love? The question nagged at her consciousness, leaving her in the wake of a steadily rising fear. Was he tiring of her already?

If so, then she was truly in a quandary of her own

making. She wanted him more than ever, and she knew that a great deal of her success in business stemmed from her dissatisfaction with their relationship. God knows she had worked herself to a standstill often enough in an attempt to forget, for a little while, the pain she and Rand were suddenly causing each other. The question was academic, in any case. She saw no way out of their dilemma, short of her giving in and allowing herself to become dependent on Rand, and that was something she couldn't do.

The disgusted sound that emerged from her throat held a core of irony. Why did she refuse to admit the truth, even to herself? She depended on Rand for the very air she breathed, and yet the admission held no hope for their future together. He wanted more from her than she was able to give. Although at times she ached with the need to declare her love for him, she remained silent. She had given him as much of an emotional commitment as she was capable of giving; yet, she felt he wanted more. Although he had ceased mentioning marriage, her refusal was still between them like a festering wound. Even their passion for each other seemed to be affected by her need to remain independent. If their desire waned, what would be left to hold them together? Heaven alone knew how little else they had in common!

The metal clang of the janitor's cleaning cart made her jump, and she summoned a smile for the elderly man who offered her a cheery greeting, which she absently returned. "Hello, Mike."

"'Lo, Ms. Benedict," he responded, shaking his

grizzled head as he pushed both the lumbering cart and himself through the narrow doorway. "I thought you'd be long gone by now."

"Why so surprised, Mike? We usually meet in passing, you know."

He chuckled and shifted the thick wad of tobacco in his mouth to the opposite cheek. "Yep, and I make sure my wife hears all about you, Ms. Benedict. My, don't she fly at me when I start bragging how the prettiest gal around takes time to talk to a rheumaticky geezer like me."

The bulge beneath the wrinkled cheek made him look more than ever like a wizened gnome, and Sara's eyes twinkled appreciatively. "One of these days your teasing is going to cost you, Mike. Mercy is going to let go with that frying pan she threatened you with the last time you brought her in, and you'll have only yourself to blame for the lump on your head."

He shook his head in amusement and spit in the tin can he kept secured to the side of his trolley. "Nope," he replied, a mischievous slant to the mouth he wiped with the back of his hand. "Gave the cast-iron ones to the church bazaar and bought her a set of those lightweight aluminum things."

Sara grinned, lifting two fingers in a sign of victory. "I always knew you were a brave man, Mike. I imagine Mercy was fit to be tied when you did away with her arsenal."

"Would 'a been, I 'spect," he grunted, lifting a ragged, cloth-ended dustmop from its pail and setting to work on the floor, "if'n I hadn't tied 'em up pretty as you please with a ribbon and give 'em to her for her birthday.''

Sara was reaching into the closet for her purse when Mike's words reached her. With a groan she leaned against the doorway, her eyes stricken as she checked the time on her watch. Nearly seven-thirty already, she thought, a feeling of shame causing her eyes to smart. Dear God, how could she have forgotten Rand's birthday? With a muttered farewell to Mike, Sara ran out of the office, the sound of the door slamming behind her adding an ominous echo to her hurrying steps. The elevator door stood open. She entered and slammed her finger against the Down button, only then conscious of her shaking hands.

By the time she was slipping her card in the computerized lock of their apartment door, she was an emotional wreck. How was she going to find the nerve to ask Rand to forgive her for spoiling their plans to celebrate, when she couldn't forgive herself? Crossing the marble-tiled foyer that opened out into a cream-color carpeted living room area of gigantic proportions, she called his name. Only silence greeted her, and after glancing outside at the balcony, for once not a whit enthralled with the panoramic view of the bay in the distance, she hurried toward their bedroom.

Rand wasn't there, and neither was he in any of the guest bedrooms, the kitchen, his den, or the roof garden that housed the swimming pool and sauna. She had practically broken every speed limit in the city, sick with remorse for her selfish preoccupation, and he hadn't even bothered to come home! Slowly retracing her steps to their bedroom, she entered the dressing area they shared and looked at the two tickets to the San Francisco Symphony she'd taped to the mirror. Her eyes filled with tears, but she refused to give in to her emotions.

Why was she standing here, regretting an evening that had probably been doomed from the onset? Her chin tilted mulishly, and with a harsh exclamation she grabbed the tickets and threw them into the wastebasket. She would shower, change, and join her friends at the Overland. At least there she could be sure of a few hours spent in congenial company. The new cyclamen blouse she'd bought for her evening with Rand was chosen in a spirit of defiance. The ankle-length skirt she'd planned to wear with it was too formal, since most of her friends would still be in their working clothes. After pulling on a pair of slacks, she strapped on matching black sandals and stood to survey her image in the mirrored doors leading into the walk-in closet.

Sara swallowed, her eyes moving from her feet to the plunging neckline of the blouse. Meant to be worn without a bra, the bodice hugged every inch of her upper body like a second skin. She swallowed again, this time with more difficulty. Worn with the long skirt, the outfit had seemed elegant. But now, Sara wasn't too sure. Teamed with the currently fashionable slacks in a clinging knit fabric, her attire seemed rather more provocative than she'd planned.

She started to remove her clothes, but her hands halted in midair. Rand was always urging her to buy clothes more suited to her femininity, she thought angrily. What difference did it make if he wasn't around to enjoy the result? Thus reassured, Sara quickly put on her makeup and brushed out her long hair. She had planned to wear it down to float over her back the way Rand liked it, and she saw no reason to change her mind. With a last rebellious glance at her reflection in the mirror, she walked out of the empty apartment.

10

·❀❀❀❀❀❀❀❀❀❀·

As usual the Overland was packed with humanity in varying stages of intoxication. Refusing to be intimidated by the crush of people, Sara pushed her way through the crowd while her eyes searched for a familiar face. It was a feat almost impossible to accomplish unless wearing stilts, she thought, whirling indignantly when a wandering hand pinched her rear. All the male faces close enough to be the culprit wore bland expressions, so she glared at all of them in turn. To her dismay a randy gleam lighted the eye of a tall, raffishly attractive individual, and as he approached her she was convinced he was the phantom pincher.

"Sara, we're over here!"

At the sound of a familiar voice, Sara's breath escaped in a whoosh of relief. With a haughty stare at her disappointed protagonist, she struggled to reach the window alcove that boasted one of the few tables in the room. Stepping onto the raised wooden floor, she returned the smiles of two of her firm's youngest executives as they rose to their feet to greet her. Paul, a blond, blue-eyed charmer who was a self-proclaimed lover of women, offered her his chair and went in search of a replacement.

"We didn't think you were coming tonight."

The remark came from Barry, the shy computer expert who ran his department with a competent efficiency she admired. She liked Barry, she thought not for the first time. He wasn't brash like Paul, and his serious nature was like her own. She turned to him with real warmth in her expression and shrugged with assumed indifference. "I changed my mind."

"I'm glad you did," he said quietly.

She flushed at the sincerity in his voice. She knew Barry found her attractive, something he hadn't tried to hide even after learning of her relationship with Rand. It was there in his gentle brown eyes whenever he looked at her, and until now she'd done her best to pretend his attraction to her didn't exist. But somehow tonight was different, and she found herself responding to the affection in his steady gaze. "To be honest, Rand changed my mind for me."

His sympathetic gaze overcame her customary desire to guard her privacy, and she found herself telling Barry more than she'd intended. "Sometimes," she admitted, "I feel like a squirrel in a cage, scurrying around and around on a wheel with no clear idea of my direction."

"You're no pet to be locked behind gilded bars, Sara," he said, his eyes intense as he leaned closer to her. "You're extremely capable of controlling your own life."

"Am I?"

He winced at her caustic reply and looked at her hand, where it lay on the table. It was curled into a defensive fist, and with a barely perceptible pause he covered it with his own. "You sound fed up."

She accepted the stroke of his fingers on the back of her knuckles, admitting to herself the overwhelming need she had for the compassion he offered. "I'm losing him, Barry," she choked, "and I don't know what to do about it."

"You love him a great deal, don't you?"

Before she could reply Paul returned with a chair held victoriously over his head. He glanced from her to Barry, sensitive to the intimate atmosphere that surrounded them. But when his eyes lowered deliberately to their linked hands, Sara drew back hurriedly, not at all happy with the conclusion Paul had drawn. A surge of color flowed under her skin, but she met the other man's speculative gaze with what little poise she had remaining. "You look pretty silly standing there with a chair over your head."

Paul, a perennial tease, wasn't about to relinquish his advantage. "I'm wondering whether to sit down or not," he said, a question in the glance he threw in Barry's direction.

"Don't be a fool," Barry muttered through gritted teeth.

The chair landed on the floor with a thud, and Paul grinned as he straddled it and draped his arms across the back. "Want to see my imitation of a gooseberry?"

Paul crossed his eyes, and his cheeks bulged. Barry scowled, but Sara couldn't contain her reaction to his clowning. Her amusement poured forth in peal after peal of laughter, and soon even the disappointed Barry couldn't prevent an appreciative grin from curving his mouth. Leaning to the side, he placed his arm across Sara's heaving shoulders. His mouth drew close to her ear as he whispered, "Don't encourage the fool!"

Sara wiped her streaming eyes and abruptly froze. There, not twenty feet away from them stood Rand, an expression on his face that almost stopped her heart. Before he lowered his lids to shield his eyes, her numbed brain registered his anger as well as his contempt. Barry, following the direction of her widening gaze, quickly removed his arm. Realizing how suspect the abrupt withdrawal must have looked to the man approaching them, she flinched inwardly.

The next few minutes passed in a blur for Sara. Dreading a scene, she was relieved when Rand showed an exceptional degree of forbearance, considering she'd been found in a bar, cuddled up to a man he'd never met before. She made the necessary introductions, her trembling voice in no way able to match his for self-control. He greeted her companions with a suave composure that alleviated their nervousness, and only she was aware of the rage hidden beneath his surface sophistication. He pulled her up to stand beside him with a proprietary hand around her waist, and barely leashed emotion leapt between them. When she feared she would no longer be able to control her shaking limbs, he glanced down at her with lips curved in a smile for the benefit of their audience, but his eyes were deadly.

"Ready to head for home, babe?"

Paul, flushed with drink and exhilaration at having at last met a man he had long emulated, protested their departure. "Hey, Sara hasn't even been here long enough to have a drink. Why don't I find another chair so you can join us?"

The smile that spread across Rand's face held a hint of malice, although the other man didn't seem to notice. Barry, however, looked worriedly at Sara. Catching the exchange of glances, Rand's fingers tightened painfully against her waist. "I'm afraid we'll have to decline your invitation, Mr. Shipley. It's my birthday, and I'm looking forward to celebrating tonight with my . . . with Sara."

The innuendo was obvious and humiliating. Without a word Sara turned, her head high as she made for the door. She sensed Rand behind her, but upon reaching the street she didn't bother to turn to him with useless recriminations. Her pain and sense of betrayal went too deep for words, and it was all she could do to swallow lungfuls of the ocean-laden breeze as she searched the parking lot for her car.

Rand, too, didn't seem to feel the urge to communicate. Seeing Sara safely inside her compact Toyota, he leaned against the hood as she secured her seat belt. "I'll follow you home."

"Yes, master," she mumbled as he threw the lock on the door and slammed it shut. She didn't think he'd heard her until she glanced through her side window and saw the mocking twist to his lips as he walked away.

Turning the key in the ignition, Sara moistened her dry lips with the tip of her tongue. As she watched Rand's long-legged stride skirt the rows ahead of her in search of his car, she longed for that drink she'd never gotten around to ordering. Releasing the hand brake and easing out of her parking space, she paid the attendant at the gate while keeping one eye on the rearview mirror. When she saw the silver-blue Porsche pull in behind her, she felt about as confident of escaping what was to come as a kitten held fast between the paws of a tiger.

Sara didn't know what to expect when Rand followed her into their apartment. Certainly she wasn't prepared for the arms that reached out to lift her against a broad chest, or the mouth that burned a path across the skin exposed at the neckline of her blouse. She sensed a wildness in Rand she'd never encountered before, and by the time he'd carried her into the bedroom and kicked the door shut behind them, she was trembling uncontrollably.

But when Rand felt the shaking of her body, all the anger seemed to drain from his features. With a careful consideration that brought tears to her eyes he lowered her onto the bed. Slowly, he straightened, the blank expression in his eyes effectively placing a barrier between them that only her explanations could bridge. Sara felt herself crushed by his unspoken recriminations and hurried into speech. "Rand, you're wrong if you think . . ."

"It doesn't matter, Sara."

Sara's heart sank at the tonelessness of the remark. Obviously, seeing her tonight with another man's arms around her, however innocent the incident or public the surroundings, had left him stripped of pride. Behind the gravel mask of his face was pain, and disillusion, and an anguish that reached out to the depths of her soul. With a strangled cry she rose to her knees, her arms reaching out to him. "Oh, God," she sobbed, pressing her forehead against his chest. "Don't look at me like that."

His body tensed, but he made no move to hold her. "How am I looking at you, Sara?"

"As though I were a nasty bug you're longing to step on."

The childish example served to ease some of the tension between them, and Rand's explosive sigh was rueful as he tilted her chin back and met her eyes. "I came on pretty strong just now," he said, his jaw tightening as he spoke. "I'm surprised you're not as disgusted with me as I am with myself."

She cupped his cheek in her hand. The tears finally overflowed her eyes when his lips kissed her palm. "I'm the one who should be ashamed, Rand. When I got home tonight and you weren't here, I think I went a little crazy. I wanted to show you I didn't care that you'd forgotten about me, so I decided to join the others at the Overland."

"What do you mean, I wasn't here?" he asked. "I came home early and waited for you until nearly eight o'clock. When you didn't show, I drove around for a while and finally decided to check the Overland. I was looking forward to our evening together. It's been so long since we've been out together, the two of us alone."

"Oh, Rand, I'm so sorry!"

She bit down hard on her lower lip, her eyes eloquent with remorse. "An unscheduled board meeting was organized, and by the time it ended I . . ."

He took a single step back, his voice guarded as he said, "I understand, Sara."

"But you don't!" She looked down, unable to meet his eyes. "It was almost a relief when you weren't here, and I could ease my own conscience by blaming you."

He hesitated, and a muscle throbbed in his cheek. "Did you arrange to meet that guy there, Sara . . . the one who was holding you when I walked in?"

"Barry's just a friend from work, Rand."

"He's more than half in love with you," he contradicted harshly. "I saw the way he was looking at you tonight."

"I've never encouraged him," she replied quietly, lifting her other hand to smooth his cheeks between her palms. "I thought several of the women in my department would be there tonight, or I wouldn't have gone. You know how impulsively I react when my temper gets the best of me. But I would never try to get back at you by dating other men. You should know that."

"I do know it," he admitted quietly.

Sara smiled. But when she received no response from Rand, the smile faltered, dying completely when he gently removed her hands from his face and moved away from her. She stared at his averted profile in disbelief, chilled by the solemnity of his expression. "Rand, I . . ."

"Wait, Sara!"

He gestured her to silence, drawing a deep breath into his lungs while his fingers massaged the tenseness from the back of his neck. "Before you say anything more, I want you to listen to me."

Sara's mouth compressed, the intensity of his gaze capturing her attention with devastating results. She began to shiver with a chill of dread, the headache pounding against her temples increasing with every breath she drew into her lungs. She wanted to plead with him for an understanding she felt she didn't deserve, and yet the only words that emerged from her mouth were defensive, a guard against the pain she sensed was inevitable. "All right, I'm listening."

"We're no good for each other, Sara."

She stiffened, anguished disbelief in the angle of her body. "I don't know how you can say that!"

"Because it's true," he replied tiredly. "Once I . . ."

He muttered an expletive, and shook his head. "Don't make this any more difficult for me than it already is, honey."

"What are you talking about?"

His shoulders straightened just seconds before he turned his head to look at her. "I'm talking about dignity, and pride, and self-respect, Sara. They're more than just words, and tonight I realize how close I came to forfeiting any right to the principles they represent. Our relationship is on self-destruct, and it has been from the beginning. We've got to let go before we end up destroying everything we once valued in each other."

With measured steps he crossed the room and hesitated in the doorway. "I'm through trying to hold on to what never really belonged to me, sweet Sara," he whispered in broken accents.

Bereft of words, Sara watched as Rand disappeared from her sight. It was then she discovered the true meaning of desolation as she heard the front door close behind the man she loved.

Sara sat curled in the fetal position on the couch and watched the first fingers of light herald a new day. A day without Rand, an inner voice whispered, and she shivered at the thought. Wrapping her arms around her midriff for warmth, she stared through the plate-glass window while an image of Rand's face as she'd last seen him rose in her mind. There had been so much pain in his eyes and a defeated droop to his broad shoulders when he walked away from her.

After he left the apartment Sara had experienced a gamut of emotions. Grief, anger, fear, and finally despair were her companions through the long hours of the night, and now she lay aching in both body and spirit. At one point she had considered packing some clothing and begging a bed for the night from either Patty or Freddie, but hope that Rand would return had kept her pacing through the apartment. Their relationship couldn't end like this, she thought. They had given too much of themselves to each other to simply walk away at the first sign of difficulty.

That was when she realized that tonight had been a culmination of the problems that had been with them from the beginning. From the first there had been signs of trouble, but she had blanked them out of her mind. She hadn't had the courage to face up to reality, and instead had lived day to day within a fantasy world. Dear God, she thought as realization opened her eyes to a truth hidden behind fear. Rand had found the courage to trust her with his love, and not once had she returned the gift. She had been too frightened of commitment to verbalize her feeling for him, and as a result she had forced Rand to exist in an emotional wasteland.

Why had she convinced herself that his avowals of love were uttered out of a need to justify their relationship? Why hadn't she remembered Rand's past and known that a man who had spent all of his life without the love he craved would never have cheapened the emotion by pretense? She had been the one to cheapen their relationship . . . and why? Because you were terrified of loving and losing Rand the way you did Sam, an inner voice answered.

Sara closed her eyes as she faced up to her own failure. As a child she was addicted to fairy tales and spent many happy hours on her father's knee, absorbing "happily ever afters." But then Sam had died, and she'd stopped believing in anything but herself. Like a greedy child, she'd pulled at Rand with one hand while pushing him away with the other. Only when they made love was she able to break through the barriers she'd placed between them, and even then she'd never been able to bring herself to return his whispered words of love and need.

She had inwardly admitted her love for Rand, but she had never stopped fighting against the dependence that love brought. She hadn't wanted to need him for her happiness, and as a result she had closed off a large portion of herself from the man who loved her. She had never once considered how difficult it must have been for Rand to admit his feelings. All of his life he had been used, first by his parents as a means to stay in his grandfather's good graces, and then by the old man himself, who had sought a form of immortality through his grandson. Rand had grown up with loneliness and a crippling lack of affection. That was why he'd been drawn to the home she and her father shared, and that was why he had clung so hard to her when Sam died.

Sweet heaven, she thought, biting down on her lower lip until it bled. In so many ways Rand had tried to show her how much he needed her in his life, and she'd been too blind with resentment to understand. She had accused him of playing God with her future, when all the while he had been trying to hold on to the only love he had ever known. Rand had needed her to need him, and she'd failed him in the cruelest way possible. She had used him to satisfy her emotional needs without giving him anything in return!

If only she had given Rand what he needed, how different this last month together would have been. Rand wouldn't have felt threatened by her career, and she wouldn't have needed to prove her independence at the expense of their love for each other. Rising slowly to her feet, Sara walked over to the sliding glass door. Opening it, she stepped onto the balcony and stared up at the stars which still fought off the break of dawn.

She was standing on the brink of an emotional chasm, invaded by a numbing sensation slowly seeping into her soul, and she desperately fought her ominous thoughts. There was a darkness reaching out for her that she still had to face, that threatened to wrap her in a silken black web of forgetfulness, and as she blinked to clear her vision she thrust her head back to search the heavens for a clue to the identity she felt slipping away from her. If she had known the truth, she wondered, would she have denied it the way she had denied Rand's love for her?

"I don't know."

Even as the wind snatched away the murmured admission, the mists finally lifted from her mind, and Sara saw herself shorn of all pretense. She at last embraced her pain with the same fervor as the gaze she kept trained on the stars. They're surrounded by the darkness, she thought, and yet they shine with a purity that provides its own light. A long time ago her eyes had burned just as brightly with anticipation of the future, she realized. But then Sam had died, and the light of hope had gone with him. She had become frightened of loving, terrified of committing herself to Rand for fear of someday losing him the way she had lost Sam.

Through her own callous indifference, the lines of communication between her and Rand had been severed. He had accepted the impermanence of their relationship because she had given him no choice, and suddenly Sara realized that by becoming Rand Emory's woman she had nearly destroyed them both. Oh, God! Why had she blinded herself to his need and seen him only through her own eyes? She had viewed his desire to marry her as one of expediency, a way to satisfy the responsibility he felt toward his friend's daughter. But her defiance had really stemmed from a lack of trust in Rand and her own insecurity.

But she was insecure no longer! She was Sara Benedict, daughter of a man who had given his love unselfishly and had it returned a thousandfold. Without Sam to guide her she had almost forgotten the lessons she had learned from her life with him. Now, as one memory slipped from her mind to be replaced by another, she was purged of the loneliness that had haunted her for so long. With an inward tremor she listened to the sigh of the wind and felt Sam's presence like a benediction.

Death had claimed her father, but he'd never really left her, she realized. He was as much a part of her life as he'd ever been, because of the love that still lingered on in her heart for him. Just as Rand will always be a part of me, she thought, hugging the knowledge to herself with a surge of joy. Even if it was too late to heal the wounds she'd inflicted on their relationship, she knew she had to try. To do any less would be to betray not only herself, but also the man she loved.

But first, Sara thought, she had to find him. Knowing Rand, he had probably spent the night at his office. Turning toward the bedroom, Sara strode straight to the walk-in closet and began rummaging among the hangers. By the time she decided on brown wool slacks and a honey-gold sweater, the room was in a shambles. Clothes were strewn over the dressing table, on the bed, and a few lay crumpled and forlorn on the floor. She just grimaced at the mess as she left the room, a surge of adrenaline giving added impetus to her footsteps.

Rand wasn't at work. Sara questioned the night watchman on duty and waited until eight o'clock so she could talk to his secretary. But Maggie was surprised by Rand's absence and even checked his desk to see if a note had been left for her. Maggie returned empty-handed, and Sara smiled her thanks before leaving the building to continue her search. She drove by a coffee shop where she knew Rand often had breakfast, but there was no sign of his car. As a last resort she drove to Fisherman's Wharf, hoping to see him walking along the pier. Finally, she admitted the futility of her actions. The best place to wait for Rand, she thought in growing frustration, was at home.

Sara drove into the underground garage and parked in one of the two spaces provided for the penthouse apartment. Her knees felt weak, as if they were made of jelly instead of bone, and she stepped out of her car and locked the door with hands that shook. Her eyes misted as she stared at Rand's Porsche. Thank God he's here, she thought, doubting if her courage would have lasted if she'd had to wait for him inside. An ache formed in her chest as she repeated the only words that mattered to her in that instant. Rand's home . . . he's home!

Now that she was so close to her goal, nervous tension attacked Sara. The elevator vibrated as it took her swiftly toward the top of the multistoried building, causing her stomach to churn sickeningly. The silence of the top floor hallway made her edgier than usual. She had to get hold of herself, she thought, or she wouldn't be able to talk at all by the time she confronted Rand.

Sara hesitated in the foyer after letting herself into the apartment and wiped her hands on the legs of her slacks. Her palms were damp with perspiration, and she could feel each exhalation of breath as though it were her last. Her heart sounded overly loud as she strained to hear any movement from Rand. At first no noise greeted her, and she began to move toward the living room. But she halted at the sound of a crash followed by a curse that came from Rand's den. Taking a deep breath, she crossed the foyer and opened the door.

"Hello, Rand."

The greeting was whispered to the man who leaned against the heavy oak desk in the corner of the room, an incredulous expression on his face. For endless moments they stared at each other until Rand, with an awkward twist of his body, motioned her inside. "What are you doing here?"

Sara jumped at the harshly accusatory tone, her brow furrowed in a frown. "I live here, in case you've forgotten."

"Did you come back for the rest of your clothes?"

Immediately Sara remembered the condition in which she'd left their bedroom, and she winced. Obviously, Rand thought she'd thrown enough of her clothes into a suitcase to get her by for a few days, and that she had planned to come back for the rest at her leisure. He thought she'd left him! He thought she cared so little for their relationship that she'd leave at the first sign of trouble. How could she convince him that she was through running away from love? If he was finished with her, he was going to have to tell her to go, not palm her off with vague innuendos about how wrong they were for each other!

181

With a mumbled apology Rand walked past her into the living room and immediately headed for the circular bar in the corner. "Would you like a drink?"

At nine-thirty in the morning, she thought incredulously, following him nervously. "N-no, thank you."

While he fixed himself a double Scotch, Sara searched for a sign that her presence was welcome, and not the irritation his abrupt manner seemed to suggest. But his face was giving nothing away. He seemed impervious to her presence, his attitude when he lifted the drink to his mouth so cold and distant she felt unbearable despair wrenching her apart inside.

I was wrong, she thought with a sensation of agonizing loss. He really doesn't want me here! Oh, God! Why had she left herself vulnerable to any more pain? Even with her eyes averted from his face, each beloved feature was vivid in her mind. She longed to trace the full curve of his lower lip with her finger, and inhale his scent while she pressed her lips to the hollow of his throat.

Above all, she wanted to press her naked breasts against the black hair on his chest and feel their hearts beat as one. She wanted to lie close to him in their darkened bedroom and whisper all the secrets of her lonely heart as she never had before. Oh, Rand! she cried silently. Don't send me away. Please . . . please don't send me away before I've had a chance to tell you how much I love you.

It was then she heard it, the tinkling sound of ice that drew her attention to the glass Rand held in his hand. She saw the tremor in those strong fingers and rejoiced at that single, visible sign of his vulnerability. Slowly, she lifted wary eyes to his, and she drew in a deep breath as she met the intensity of his gaze. She knew that look of hunger so well, she thought, dazed by the silver sheen of his eyes. Uttering a choked cry, she started to lessen the distance that separated them.

But Rand turned away and put his drink down. He kept his back to her while he wiped his damp hand on a bar towel.

"Why are you here, Sara?" he asked. "Do we have to drag the end out to the utmost?"

"Because there is no end to the way I feel about you, Rand."

"What kind of game are you playing now? Are you hoping to see me crawl?"

Sara's eyes widened. "Do you think me so cruel?" she gasped, twisting her hands together to stop their trembling.

His eyes narrowed on her distraught features. "What the hell do you care what I think or feel?"

"I care," she whispered, her expression pleading for his understanding.

"I came close to forcing myself on you last night, and I'm sick to my soul," he said, his mouth curving with cynical mockery. "Does it give you a thrill to know you've stripped me of all dignity, Sara?"

"I was the one stripped of dignity, Rand."

She took a few faltering steps toward him but found herself unable to bridge the last of the distance between them. His cynicism had struck deep, and Sara was determined not to show how much his attitude was hurting her. She slammed her hands on her hips and faced him with defiance in the angle of her jaw. "You were the one who walked away from me!"

"It was either that, or . . ." He hesitated and ran his hand through his hair as he stared down at the floor. "I was planning to vent my anger and jealousy physically, and suddenly I was sickened by my own actions. I knew then that I'd been wrong to try to make you love me by using the physical attraction between us."

"That's not true," she objected furiously. "I've always loved you, Rand!"

"Is that what you called it?"

She was shocked by his ridiculing laughter, and she resisted the urge to put her hands over her ears. On unsteady legs she walked to the sliding glass doors and looked out into a day heavy with fog. She didn't want him to see the agony in her expression. "Mockery doesn't become you, Rand. I loved you, but I was afraid to trust you. You see," she said, leaning her forehead against the cool glass and closing her eyes, "I couldn't bear losing you, too."

His voice sounded behind her. "What do you mean, Sara?"

"I discovered how much love hurts when it suddenly isn't there anymore. Sam died, and eventually you would have tired of me. There just wasn't anything but my need of you to hold us together."

"Is that why you wouldn't marry me and have my children?" he asked, his voice shaking. "You thought that someday I'd tire of you and just discard you like an old shoe? My God, you have quite an opinion of me, don't you?"

"Can't you understand? We come from different worlds. I'm a simple person, and I was always afraid I'd fail you. The only position I thought I could fulfill successfully was that of a lover. That way I didn't have to commit my whole life to you. I was so afraid of becoming just another of your possessions, not a wife in the truest sense of the word. I wanted you to need me, but I was terrified of letting myself need you. Oh, God, Rand! It's bad enough losing the person you care about most in the world to death, but it would be unbearable to lose someone to indifference. Please, don't send me away. Give me a chance to show you how much I love you."

Sara glanced behind her and with a broken cry stumbled into the arms that reached for her. "I can't send you away again," Rand said fiercely, his body trembling. "Last night, seeing you with another man, I thought you wanted to be free of me. Oh, God! You don't know how hard that was when all I wanted was to beg you to stay with me, Sara!"

"Then will you marry me, Rand?"

He tensed and drew back to look at her with disbelieving eyes. "What did you say?"

"I want to marry you, and love you, and depend on you and our children for my happiness," she whispered.

They had both been lost, she thought, but now they were where they belonged. With a smile of joy she urged him closer. His arms circled her tightly, and she felt his breathing accelerate. Then his mouth was on hers, and she opened herself to the hungry foraging of his tongue. Eagerly she unbuttoned his shirt, her hands aching for the feel of his flesh.

"Oh, honey, I need you so much!"

"Need goes hand in hand with love, doesn't it, Rand?" she remarked dreamily, curling her fingers in the dark hair on his chest until he shivered with sensation.

"I loved you as a child, as a woman, and . . ."

She pressed her hand against his mouth, her eyes wide with appeal. "Will you love me as a wife?"

"It's what I've wanted since the moment I saw you," he said, his voice breaking.

"Then let me be your woman again," she said, wrapping her arms around his neck. "Make me your woman . . . and your wife!"

With a triumphant smile Rand lifted her against his chest and carried her into the bedroom. The door closed behind them, and they returned to a world that existed only when they were together. It was a world of need, and caring, and a love so deep, it would follow them into eternity.

a fabulous $50,000
diamond jewelry collection

by filling out the coupon below
and mailing it by September 30, 1985

Send entries to:

U.S.
Silhouette Diamond Sweepstakes
P.O. Box 779
Madison Square Station
New York, NY 10159

Canada
Silhouette Diamond Sweepstakes
Suite 191
238 Davenport Road
Toronto, Ontario M5R 1J6

SILHOUETTE DIAMOND SWEEPSTAKES
ENTRY FORM

☐ Mrs.   ☐ Miss   ☐ Ms   ☐ Mr.

NAME _____ (please print)

ADDRESS _____ APT. #

CITY _____

STATE/(PROV.) _____

ZIP/(POSTAL CODE) _____

RTD-A-1

RULES FOR SILHOUETTE DIAMOND SWEEPSTAKES

OFFICIAL RULES — NO PURCHASE NECESSARY

1. Silhouette Diamond Sweepstakes is open to Canadian (except Quebec) and United States residents 18 years or older at the time of entry. Employees and immediate families of the publishers of Silhouette, their affiliates, retailers, distributors, printers, agencies and RONALD SMILEY INC. are excluded.

2. To enter, print your name and address on the official entry form or on a 3" x 5" slip of paper. You may enter as often as you choose, but each envelope must contain only one entry. Mail entries first class in Canada to Silhouette Diamond Sweepstakes, Suite 191, 238 Davenport Road, Toronto, Ontario M5R 1J6. In the United States, mail to Silhouette Diamond Sweepstakes, P.O. Box 779, Madison Square Station, New York, NY 10159. Entries must be postmarked between February 1 and September 30, 1985. Silhouette is not responsible for lost, late or misdirected mail.

3. First Prize of diamond jewelry, consisting of a necklace, ring, bracelet and earrings will be awarded. Approximate retail value is $50,000 U.S./$62,500 Canadian. Second Prize of 100 Silhouette Home Reader Service Subscriptions will be awarded. Approximate retail value of each is $162.00 U.S./$180.00 Canadian. No substitution, duplication, cash redemption or transfer of prizes will be permitted. Odds of winning depend upon the number of valid entries received. One prize to a family or household. Income taxes, other taxes and insurance on First Prize are the sole responsibility of the winners.

4. Winners will be selected under the supervision of RONALD SMILEY INC., an independent judging organization whose decisions are final, by random drawings from valid entries postmarked by September 30, 1985, and received no later than October 7, 1985. Entry in this sweepstakes indicates your awareness of the Official Rules. Winners who are residents of Canada must answer correctly a time-related arithmetical skill-testing question to qualify. First Prize winner will be notified by certified mail and must submit an Affidavit of Compliance within 10 days of notification. Returned Affidavits or prizes that are refused or undeliverable will result in alternative names being randomly drawn. Winners may be asked for use of their name and photo at no additional compensation.

5. For a First Prize winner list, send a stamped self-addressed envelope postmarked by September 30, 1985. In Canada, mail to Silhouette Diamond Contest Winner, Suite 309, 238 Davenport Road, Toronto, Ontario M5R 1J6. In the United States, mail to Silhouette Diamond Contest Winner, P.O. Box 182, Bowling Green Station, New York, NY 10274. This offer will appear in Silhouette publications and at participating retailers. Offer void in Quebec and subject to all Federal, Provincial, State and Municipal laws and regulations and wherever prohibited or restricted by law.

SDR-A-1

If you've enjoyed this book, mail this coupon and get 4 thrilling

Silhouette Desire®

novels FREE (a $7.80 value)

If you've enjoyed this Silhouette Desire novel, you'll love the 4 FREE books waiting for you! They're yours as our gift to introduce you to our home subscription service.

Get Silhouette Desire novels before they're available anywhere else.

Through our home subscription service, you can get Silhouette Desire romance novels regularly—delivered right to your door! Your books will be *shipped to you two months before they're available anywhere else*—so you'll never miss a new title. Each month we'll send you 6 new books to look over for 15 days, without obligation. If not delighted, simply return them and owe nothing. Or keep them and pay only $1.95 each. There's no charge for postage or handling. And there's no obligation to buy anything at any time. You'll also receive a subscription to the Silhouette Books Newsletter *absolutely free!*

So don't wait. To receive your four FREE books, fill out and mail the coupon below *today!*

SILHOUETTE DESIRE and colophon are registered trademarks and a service mark.

Silhouette Desire,® 120 Brighton Road, P.O. Box 5084, Clifton, N.J. 07015-5084

Yes, please send me FREE and without obligation, 4 exciting Silhouette Desire books. Unless you hear from me after I receive them, send me 6 new Silhouette Desire books to preview each month before they're available anywhere else. I understand that you will bill me just $1.95 each for a total of $11.70—with no additional shipping, handling or other hidden charges. **There is no minimum number of books that I must buy, and I can cancel anytime I wish.** The first 4 books are mine to keep, even if I never take a single additional book.

☐ Mrs. ☐ Miss ☐ Ms. ☐ Mr.

BDD3R5

Name	*(please print)*	
Address		Apt. #
City	State	Zip
( )		
Area Code	Telephone Number	

Signature (If under 18, parent or guardian must sign.)

This offer limited to one per customer. Terms and prices subject to change. Your enrollment is subject to acceptance by Silhouette Books.

DD-R-A

She fought for a bold future
until she could no longer
ignore the...

ECHO OF THUNDER

MAURA SEGER

Author of Eye of the Storm

ECHO OF THUNDER is the love story of James
Callahan and Alexis Brockton, who forge a union
that must withstand the pressures of their own
desires and the challenge of building a new television
empire.

Author Maura Seger's writing has been described by
Romantic Times as having a "superb blend of
historical perspective, exciting romance and a deep
and abiding passion for the human soul."

**Available at your favorite
retail outlet in SEPTEMBER.**

Silhouette Desire

COMING NEXT MONTH

BEYOND LOVE—Ann Major
Nine years had passed since a misunderstanding had forced Dinah to leave Morgan Hastings. Armed with the truth, Morgan set out to win her back.

THE TENDER STRANGER—Diana Palmer
After a whirlwind romance, Dani St. Clair found herself blissfully married to a man she hardly knew. Nothing could have shattered her happiness...until his dangerous secret was revealed.

MOON MADNESS—Freda Vasilos
Two years of separation had changed nothing. Jason Stephanou was still the only man capable of driving all reason from Sophie's mind. He was the one she loved. How could she leave him again?

STARLIGHT—Penelope Wisdom
An accident suddenly ended jockey Trevor Laird's career and brought her face-to-face once again with Steven Montford, the man she had always loved, and the father of a child he didn't know existed.

YEAR OF THE POET—Ann Hurley
Child psychologist Joyce Lanier had a good head on her shoulders. Little could rattle this calm professional until wild Irish poet Neill Riorden pierced her reserve and shook her to her very core.

A BIRD IN HAND—Dixie Browning
When Anny Cousins decided to take in a boarder from the nearby university, she looked forward to playing dominoes with a stodgy old professor. She was in for a big surprise!

AVAILABLE THIS MONTH

SIMPLE PLEASURES
Lynda Trent

COUNTRY BLUE
Marie Nicole

NO SENSE OF HUMOR
Elizabeth Alden

ANNA'S CHILD
Angel Milan

ALL THE MARBLES
Beverly Bird

RAND EMORY'S WOMAN
Nicole Monet